LICKING THE KNIFE
Jamie Lee Carrie

©12.04.2024 Jamie Lee Carrie LLC

All rights reserved: Licking the Knife

US Library of Congress: TXU 2-458-702

©Cover art "Allison" by J.L Carrie

ISBN: 979-8-9926590-2-3 (PB)

ISBN: 979-8-9918618-5-4 (KINDLE)

ISBN: 979-8-9926590-1-6 (EPUB)

****I am an AMERICAN author. I speak and write in the dialogue that is prevalent in the USA, specifically, in the southern states. If you are not familiar with this dialect, I do apologize. It is not considered proper KING'S ENGLISH, but it is proper spelling and grammar for my country of origin. Some phrases may have to be googled for better understanding. I hope it does not hinder your ability to read, understand, and enjoy.**

For David,
Thanks for the challenge.

Jamie Lee Carrie

~It is said that those who are not spoon-fed love learn to lick what they can from knives.

One

Allison stood over her kitchen sink, blankly staring out the window, listening to the water run. Her view was of the corner of her front yard, where her barren rosebushes stood. The end of the blooming season always felt a bit sad.

She watched as the neighbors pulled into their driveway, got out of their car, and collected their groceries and children. They were having a conversation that she couldn't hear. They looked happy, and she became lost in their unknown story for a moment.

"Allie. *ALLIE!*" Her husband's voice pulled her out of her daze, just in time to see the water overfilling the sink and starting to run down the cabinet.

"Oh shit!" She shut it off and absentmindedly started soaking up the mess.

It was her birthday, and it always frustrated her the way he planned dinner parties meant for her—that she had to organize. She had been responsible for every detail. From the food to the alcohol and guests. Yet she was supposed to feel happy over the occasion that had done nothing but consume her time for the last month.

He walked over and leaned against the counter. He had removed his suit jacket but still had on the white shirt and tie he'd worn to the office. He appeared disheveled, as he always did at that time of day. His arms were folded across his chest—in his hand was a cocktail. He spoke about a case he was working on, pausing periodically to sip his scotch.

Allie listened as she did a few dishes and cleaned up around the kitchen. The boring, monotonous dialog that seemed to be his only effort in communication for as long as she could remember. It was a ritual of sorts—his talking about himself or some high-profile criminal he was defending in any given month. It was excruciating for her to listen again and again. Same story, different day.

Honestly, she had stopped really listening ten years prior. Nodding her head at appropriate times during his rambling had become second nature.

She interrupted him.

"Heath, dear, the caterers will be here shortly. Why don't you go get showered and changed?"

He stared at her for a moment before setting his glass down and heading upstairs.

As she watched him leave the room, she felt nothing but animosity and disdain. She knew she had loved him at one point but couldn't remember when or why. Lately, she kept asking herself the same question. If she had known that her parents were wealthy before they died, would she have married him at all? She knew the answer, but it gave no relief. Instead, it just pissed her off. Created more anger for the decisions she'd made without the whole picture. She had wasted her youth and beauty on a mediocre man—a mediocre life. She felt cheated somehow.

As she draped a cup towel over the faucet, her cocker spaniel, Trixie, started her high, shrill alert bark. She heard her son holler.

"MOM?"

She greeted him in the dining room entryway.

"Benny, you're early." They exchanged a quick hug and kiss on the cheek. He was one of the few things that brought her joy anymore; seeing him always elevated her mood.

"Where's Jake?" she asked.

"First of all, happy birthday. Secondly, I

think you like him more than you like me. He can't make it; he has an exhibit this week he is going crazy over. It is going to be a big deal; it's on Saturday; you should come."

"Well, they *are* called your better half for a reason, sweetie." She teased.

Jake is Ben's life partner and a huge point of contention with Heath. He viewed their son's sexual orientation as some kind of parental failure on his part. A fact that Allison couldn't wrap her head around.

He turned around and greeted his catering crew walking up the sidewalk, then started doing what he does best: directing them.

"Ben, can I help with anything?"

"Mom, no. I've got this. Just keep Trixie out of the way and go have a drink." With a quick wink and smile, he turned his attention toward the second crew making their way in.

She bent down and scooped up the dog, and after putting her in the backyard for the time being, she poured herself a glass of chardonnay, popped a Xanax, and made her way up to enjoy her last bit of solitude before guests arrived.

Lying in the bath, she considered her world. It seemed to her that it was a reoccurring theme as of late—the rehashing of her life to that point and how she got where she was. At forty-four years old, she had a lovely home in an affluent neighborhood, a successful husband, a son she adored, many friends, and all of the comforts anyone could ask for. Then why did life seem like such a chore? She suffered with the realization that she had become a cliche.

"Fuck my life." She said it out loud and then submerged her whole body under the water to the crown of her head. The warmth felt good, and she stayed completely under as long as she could before her breath gave out. Coming up only because she needed air.

After getting out, drying her hair, applying makeup, and putting on a simple black dress and a single string of pearls, she made her way back downstairs.

Ben had outdone himself. In the short time it took her to get ready, he had transformed her formal dining room into a work of art.

Eighteen places had been set on the table using her good china, with silver cutlery set in appropriate places on either side of them. Crystal stemware accompanied each, with cloth napkins shaped into rosebuds at the head of every one. Candelabras were strategically placed down the middle of the table and on the buffet, and beautiful, enormous flower arrangements completed the scene. They were white roses and spider lilies, her favorites.

She walked around, running her hand along the side of the lengthy table, feeling the linen tablecloth beneath her fingers. With every dinner party, she felt more disconnected. This was never her wish and definitely didn't represent a good time to her. But even she recognized the beauty of it all. There was new warmth to a space that only a couple of hours earlier had been cold and uncharacteristic.

She headed into the kitchen, grabbing a gin and tonic on the way. Standing in the doorway, she watched as the final touches were being made to her birthday dinner. She noticed the time; it was 7 pm. She had about thirty minutes to get her head straight before guests arrived.

With a deep sigh and more than a decent amount of loathing, she slipped on her shoes and went to check on Trixie.

As she rounded the corner to the den, Heath intercepted her. Without asking, he said,

"No need to worry about the dog; I put her in her kennel. The last thing I need tonight is that insufferable animal jumping on guests and begging at the dinner table."

His flushed face and bloodshot eyes told her he was already drunk. If not completely, he was definitely teetering on the edge. That statement made her blood boil; she loved that animal more than she loved him, and his jealousy over that particular fact was marginally psychotic. Before she could respond, he thrust something into her hand.

Of course; it was the token birthday gift. Each year given, not for her pleasure or enjoyment but more for the show of it over dinner. Most certainly another tacky piece of jewelry.

She opened the velvet box, and no surprise to her, it was exactly that. A bracelet, encrusted with diamonds and emeralds. And although she loved both stones, she detested them because of the giver. She offered a dry,

"Thank you, dear."

He rolled his eyes and walked away. Saying,

"Nothing's ever good enough for the princess." Under his breath.

He didn't like her any more than she liked him. Coexisting with one another had become absolutely painful. She was fastening the clasp around her wrist as the first of the guests arrived.

Within an hour, she was seated at the table with seventeen people that had come to celebrate her special day. The dim room and low light from the candles gave everyone a more ghoulish appearance than she was comfortable with.

As she sat listening to the conversation, she was overwhelmed with annoyance at the mindless chatter. It was all the same people, from all of the same dinner parties, just different occasions, from the last ten years. Topics never veered further than investments, convicts, idle gossip, and basic bullshit.

It was as if the identical party was regurgitated year after year, with the absence or replacement of one or two characters. She felt contempt for every last one of them, and all she could think about was escaping to her room to smoke a joint.

But she was expected to stay and be the perfect hostess. So, like so many times before, she resigned herself to her fate and put on an act. One that she had become quite good at through the years.

Until the inevitable topic of her birthday present arose, and she had to listen to twenty minutes of facts surrounding the grade of stones, the rarity of the piece, the particular content of the gold, and of course the sought-after jeweler who had crafted it. She couldn't bear it; she had had enough. She stood, offered coffee and Cognac in the living room, and quickly led the pack to relocate before she lost her fucking mind.

After moving, everyone divided into their individual cliques and continued the evening.

There was no satisfaction in it. Not just for her, but for any of them. It seemed that getting together was used mainly as an excuse to drink way too much and voice their opinions on politics or other unsavory topics. She milled around catching tidbits of borderline arguments and philosophical debates. It was torture. Plain and simple.

She watched as Heath and two colleagues walked out into the backyard. They worked at his law firm, Smith & Kirby. She detested attorneys, and because she was married to one, she could never escape them. They just came across as a more prominent type of used car salesman. Arguing a point, blurring, or omitting the truth for financial gain and recognition. She held not one ounce of respect for any of them, including her spouse.

They were standing by the pool smoking, and the discussion they were having seemed to be heated. Heath began to use his hands to accentuate whatever point he was trying to make. She couldn't hear what it was that had him so animated. She had seen that defensive stance too many times in the last twenty years to count, but she never cared enough to get to the bottom of it. That time was no different.

She pulled her attention away and made herself another drink. Biding time until the evening could draw to its long overdue close.

It was after eleven when the last of them left. She made a beeline to the kennel and took Trixie straight to the back door to let her out. She must have been ready to burst.

After going upstairs to wash her face and change, she donned her robe and went back down for a nightcap. To complete the last of her normal responsibilities, she found her pillbox, noted the day, and dumped the entire contents into her palm. She put the whole handful in her mouth and chased them with what was left of an open bottle of wine sitting on the counter. She looked forward to that time of day all day, every day.

Afterwards, she took a habitual stroll through her art studio. The room was just off of the kitchen, and it had become a much-needed part of her routine. It reeked of imported vanilla linseed oil, and somehow it gave her comfort to smell the paint and study her projects, especially the incomplete ones. She lingered over her latest work. It was a painting of Ben and Trixie from just before his high school graduation. He was the only success she could boast in her lifetime, and it made her smile—the pride she felt in him. That feeling was quickly accompanied by overwhelming melancholy. The portrait was from happier days gone by that she couldn't get back.

As she reached up to feel the canvas, the bracelet slid up towards her elbow, reminding her of its presence. The clasp couldn't be undone without help, and she was stuck with it. Attached to her like barnacles on a ship. Reminding her of the proverbial weight around her neck. *Disgusting.*

She shuddered as she turned out the light, left the room, and closed the door behind her. Limiting access to her sacred space, if only in a small way.

It was then that she realized Heath wasn't around. With that epiphany, her whole body relaxed. She felt relief at his absence and just assumed he'd snuck off to meet his newest mistress. It didn't bother her.

On the contrary, it brought her immense comfort to know she wouldn't have to endure his drunken advances. Having sex with him was unimaginative and tiresome; she preferred to do without. He approached sex the same way he did with everything else in his life—straightforward and planned. It was a necessary duty with a needed outcome; that was it—no more, no less.

She poured herself a highball of gin, foregoing the usual ice or tonic, and walked around shutting off lights, choosing to enjoy it in the living room. She sat in a chair by her bay window, the only light coming from the pool, illuminating just enough to give the room a dreamlike quality. She leaned back and closed her eyes, relishing the first bit of peace she'd had in days.

She was drawn out of her relaxed state and abruptly shaken into the present by Trixie's yelp. Not her normal bark, but a painful cry. Allison jolted up immediately, dropping her glass and spilling its contents all over her lap. She stood to walk to the door and had to steady herself on the table beside her. Something *was wrong*.

It felt as if all of the blood had rushed to her head, causing the room to spin. The furniture seemed to be moving around her; the floor was shaking beneath her feet.

After gaining a bit of stability, she took a few steps. Each one taking all of her concentration, each one more of a struggle. It was an incredible amount of work just to get to her intended destination, knocking over a standing lamp in the short distance. She stood in the doorway, using the frame for stability. Her mind was foggy, as if spiderwebs had replaced her brain somehow; her mouth was full of cotton.

She instinctively felt that she was not alone and scanned the lounge area surrounding the pool. She saw no one, but in her peripheral vision, movement. A dark shadow that seemed to blur back into the outside wall of the house. She stepped down onto the pavement and lost her footing, causing her to fall and end up on all fours.

Narrowing her eyes and looking in the direction of the water, she observed something floating in it. She felt asleep, but with the absolute knowledge that she was, in fact, awake.

Unable to stand back up, she crawled along the concrete to the rim of the pool. Each movement was exhausting and took every ounce of energy she possessed. Peering over the edge, she tried to focus.

So much effort to do something her eyes should have known to do on their own.

There, floating in the water, was Trixie. She couldn't make sense of what she was seeing and couldn't put her thoughts into any kind of collective order. Confusion enveloped her as she tried to speak. Only whispers came back to her own ears.

Lying on her stomach, reaching for her beloved pet, she felt herself begin to fall in. And then arms surrounded her, pulling her up and out. Her limbs weighed so much, her head felt so heavy, and her own voice sounded as if it were being relayed through a tube or tunnel.

She looked up and into a face she had never seen before, hovering above her. A large, dark man with strong features, black eyes, and a hollow stare.

There was no fight in her; all of her effort wouldn't manifest the reaction she wanted or needed. Darkness kept creeping in, forcing its way around her pupils, like charcoal paint droplets in water, swirling around along the edges of her eyes.

It was trying to engulf her, and she fought to keep it at bay. A futile attempt at retaining some kind of control that she had somehow lost in those last few minutes.

She was being carried and felt the magnitude of her own dead weight. She was too confused to feel the fear that should have been primal. The only sound was that of her own voice reassuring her on a loop, "It's all a dream, Allison; it's all just a dream."

Without having a decision about anything that was playing out before her eyes and in her head, she forfeited her imagined power and let go of her consciousness.

All at once, succumbing and sinking into the dark abyss.

Two

Leo pulled the dark blue Audi off of the highway and onto the first country road he approached. He came to a stop, and after consulting Maps, he was satisfied he was going the best way.

He took a few extra moments to observe his surroundings, looking for unwelcome headlights or movement before getting out to check on his new travel companion. After grabbing the syringe from his toiletry case and popping the trunk, he made his way to the back of the car. Again, surveying the area before completely opening it.

Standing there looking at her with only the dim lighting coming from the car, it was hard to believe that she was the same woman he had followed the last few months. She had been his mark and the center of his attention for as long as he could remember, and there she was, helpless in the trunk. One of the final steps to a perfectly executed plan to end his troubles.

He pondered a bit too long over that fact before jabbing the medicine into her arm. A necessary assurance that the rest of the trip would be uneventful. He covered her again with a blanket, threw the syringe into the brush, and then settled back in the driver's seat.

He had about seven hours to get from Washington to Oregon. He needed to get across state lines before sunrise, when she would be reported missing. He intended to stay on smaller back roads and off of the interstate the whole trip, lessening the probability of traffic cameras. It was the only thing he felt sure of in all of it— his ability to remain unseen. He was counting on it.

Being grateful for her excellent taste in cars, he adjusted the seat, turned on the heater and the radio, and continued to his destination.

Months of planning hadn't prepared him for the anxiety he was feeling. Even though he knew everything was going as expected, he still kept reevaluating to the point of obsession. He was hyper-focused on each step, and it likely wouldn't stop until she was deposited safely in the cabin he'd made ready for her incarceration.

This was a habit that had always served him well—the attention to every minute detail. Which was good, because he didn't see himself changing anytime soon. He was who he was and had learned to use it to his benefit.

Mile after mile went by with only his thoughts to occupy his head, and they varied from which step he was on in the overall plan to what he was facing in the very near future. He had agreed to kill her, and there was no backing out.

He tried in vain to dismiss that particular image, but the more he tried, the more it engrossed him. It became much more disturbing to him with each passing hour. He shifted his mind to his father instead. In hopes that if once again, he took into account the reasoning behind what he was doing, it would offer him some peace.

Leo and his family were from Israel. They were part of the Muslim minority there and had moved to the United States when he was seven in search of a better life. His father, though considered a peaceful man, had gotten himself into trouble. In all actuality, they'd left in the middle of the night in secrecy with only the clothes on their backs and plane fare purchased by shady business associates. It had taken every bit of the first twenty years in America to get established and only the last five to unravel. His father had a knack for getting involved in impossible situations. Situations that, at that point, only Leo could get him out of.

He inhaled and let out a deep sigh. Rehashing everything wasn't helping. The fact was that the people that his new captive's husband owed were the exact same people that his father did. This was a way to make his family square across the board. It was the only chance for freedom, and his mother and little sister didn't deserve what would happen if he chose not to carry out the plan. He had no choice. If he failed now, it would mean death for all of them. He wasn't doing it for family honor; he was doing it for survival.

Disposing of a middle-aged, spoiled, and miserable woman would save four lives. And the way he looked at it, he was probably doing her a favor.

He lit a cigarette and mulled over the parts of her life he'd seen recently.

He had watched her come and go. Always the same mundane tasks. The market, bookstore, dry cleaners, shopping, and dinner parties. Morning jogs at 5 am like clockwork. No real friends or meaningful activities that would be considered worthwhile or proof of good character. Her husband was a piece of shit who frequented hotels with a whole roster of different women, and the only thing she seemed to have love or compassion for was her dog. A dog that was now dead—something he did feel bad about. Although he hadn't been the one to kill her faithful companion, he had stood by and watched as her neck was broken. Reaffirming what he assumed about her husband—that he was a cold-hearted coward.

He thought about an occasion only two days before when he had watched Allison in her studio. It was late evening, and he was intrigued as she stood for hours focused on a piece of canvas. She looked calm, and it was the closest hint of happiness he had seen from her.

When she was painting, she took on a different aura. Something he could even see through the window, peering out from behind the high shrubbery.

He shook his head, trying to snap himself out of it. He couldn't view her as a person. Not now, not ever. He had a job to do, and in three weeks it would all be behind him.

The rest of the drive took less time than he had anticipated, and he pulled onto the nondescript dirt road a few hours past sunrise. He wound down through the trees slowly for over an hour to prevent damage to the undercarriage of the Audi and parked next to his Jeep. After going into the cabin to turn everything on and start a fire, he went back to get her. He could smell urine. As he picked her up and carried her into the house, he again felt a twinge of guilt over his manner of transporting her.

He carried her to the bedroom and

unwrapped the blanket. She was wearing a simple robe, black lace undies, and a matching bra. All soaked, as well as the front of his jeans and shirt. The smell was nauseating.

The water heater hadn't been on for weeks, and the water from the tap was freezing. He removed the tape from across her mouth and left her there sprawled out on the cold floor while he contemplated what to do.

After giving it some thought, he heated water on the stove, cleaned himself up, and changed, then returned to the room with a pan of warm soapy water and a spare flannel shirt.

It took all of his concentration to be mechanical and deliberate in his actions, and after removing her soiled undergarments, he lingered over her for a moment. He considered her. For the first time, he found himself really looking at her. Unhindered and unhurried.

She was beautiful. Her body looked to be that of a young woman. Legs long and lean, breasts still exceptional, and skin that had never seen a hard day in the sun; fair and milky in its appearance next to his. She had the attributes belonging to someone of obvious privilege. Soft, supple, and cared for. And yet he felt no animosity or anger.

He stayed there on his knees, scanning her from head to toe, memorizing every freckle, dimple, and all of her bits of perfection. Lying there in front of him, she seemed to embody everything opposite of how he had previously viewed her. Her femininity overwhelmed him.

Each stroke with the warm washcloth left a trail of goose bumps behind. Her whole body became covered with ripples. He brushed her sandy blond hair out of her face and ran his thumb across her bottom lip. Still, there was no movement at all, and it was starting to worry him.

He leaned over her, positioning his ear over her mouth. She was breathing.

He felt relieved, and then he felt foolish. An accidental overdose would have saved him the trouble.

He dressed her in his flannel that all but swallowed her, buttoned it up, and carried her to the bed. He secured her hands and feet and covered her with a heavy blanket.

He removed and pocketed her ornate gold bracelet and left the room.

***

Allison woke up in her mind long before she opened her eyes. Her head was pounding, accompanied by a metallic taste in her mouth, and her hands were cold. Instinctively, she pulled her arms down to put them under the covers and realized pretty quickly that she couldn't. Something was holding them in place. Trying then to pull her knees up to her chest and roll over.

That was impossible as well, and she thought herself dreaming.

Again she tried, and upon the second failure, she slowly opened her eyes.

Lying for a moment, looking around at the unfamiliar surroundings, she was completely confused. She tried to look up and see what was holding her arms, but the position of the pillow made it impossible. She arched her back, and tilting her chin up, she could finally see what she was tethered to.

On both of her wrists were leather cuffs; attached to those were rings and short chains connected to a long iron rod that ran the width of the bed. Looking down, she was covered with a quilt but could only assume her ankles were in the same setup. They allowed her to slightly bend her elbows and move her limbs side to side but not up and down. Without thought to why, she started doing just that. First the right arm, and then the left. She repeated it with her legs.

As realization set in, she stopped and listened. All she could hear were loud thumps, seeming to come from outside.

Looking around the room, it was a cabin of some sort, with plank walls and rudimentary furnishings. There were two doors, both to her left, but she had no idea what they led to. A double window high on the wall to her right was covered with heavy drapes, and she could see beams of light coming in around them. On a far wall was a dresser, but nothing else significant.

Fear washed over her, and she wasn't sure what to do with herself.

She tried to remember the night before, but the last thing she could recall was the guests leaving after the dinner party. Had it even been the night before? She had no idea what day it was, and no matter what she tried to focus on, her mind kept going back to the same scene. Her birthday dinner was the last thing she had a clear memory of. How had she gotten where she was, and why?

She licked her lips with a dry tongue that felt twice its normal size and started to speak. As if the sound of her own voice would somehow make the situation more real. At first, nothing came. She cleared her throat and started again. "Hello?" came out in a whisper. She repeated it. "Hello."

Nothing. No change in her surroundings, and no one coming. No human acknowledgment of her. The magnitude of her situation hit her all at once. She found herself in a frenzy and started to scream.

"What in the fuck is going on? HELP! SOMEBODY HELP!"

Along with reckless pleas spilling out of her were sounds made up of no real words. The kind of screams that escape someone when true fear takes over. The kind that makes no real sense but relays exactly what they need to. As if falling from a cliff, full of adrenaline, grabbing at the air when the ground is coming quickly. No escape and no recourse, except her own voice. A voice that kept getting louder with each attempt.

She heard a door slam and heavy footsteps making their way across the wooden floor. She stopped to listen. They were coming towards her.

The farthest doorway opened, and a man appeared. She narrowed her eyes, and a flash of a dream played out in her mind. Somehow, he seemed familiar. Somewhere deep in her subconscious, she recognized him. He stood, wordless, for a moment. They were both silently staring at one another.

He was wearing a white shirt, and lines of sweat glistened and trickled down his neck and along the edges of his face. His breathing was quick and shallow, as if he had been doing some type of hard labor. He walked towards her.

In a raspy voice that seemed more like a growl, he said,

"There is no use screaming; we are far away from anyone who could hear you. But if you choose to continue, I will tape your mouth closed. That is my first and last warning."

Allison gave him the most intimidating look she could muster before speaking.

"Why am I here? If it is money you're after, I have plenty. Just tell me what you want."

He had to stifle a chuckle at her first words.

Simply because it was no surprise to him. Rich people always felt money would fix everything, no matter what it was. His nonchalant attitude infuriated her. Which was also no surprise.

"I don't know who you are or what this is about, but you messed with the wrong woman. My husband is a very powerful man. He will find me, and he will have you killed."

Leo was busy checking the leather straps around her ankles. Her feet were turning a light shade of blue, so he unlocked and loosened each in turn before looking up at her and answering.

"This is temporary; I have no wish to hurt you. You will be safely returned to your family eventually, but only if you don't do anything stupid. Stay calm, and do not make me regret leaving your mouth and eyes uncovered."

No matter his cold manner in delivery of them, his words gave her a small amount of relief, and her body relaxed a little.

"I have to pee." She told him.

He hesitated a moment, then reached under the bed and pulled out a porcelain bedpan, and she immediately regretted needing to go.

"*No fucking thank you*, I'll wait."

He raised one eyebrow and gave her a stern look before pulling back the covers, lifting her bottom, and placing the bedpan under her. He seemed annoyed and said,

"Don't be ridiculous."

He left for a few minutes, came back and wiped her with a warm rag, then returned her to her original position. Again, covering her with the blanket.

He opened the other door in the room and disappeared behind it. She could hear a toilet flush and water running from a sink. And then he left.

"Bastard!" She said as he closed the door behind him.

Three

Allison laid awake for a while after he left. She looked around, taking everything into account. Her mind was trying to develop a plan of some kind. She sure in hell wasn't going to just accept the fact she was a prisoner, chained to a bed and at that stranger's disposal.

It felt like hours alone, her mind racing but coming up with no solution. Her eyes became heavy, and she couldn't keep them open.

She wasn't sure how long she had dozed before she heard the door open again.

He came back in carrying a tray, and she smelled coffee before he even made it across the room. He laid the tray down on the nightstand and pulled the blanket up to her knees. As he put his hands on the left ankle cuff, he paused and looked her directly in the eyes.

"I am going to release your ankles so that you can sit up and eat. I am warning you now not to do anything you'll regret. Do you understand?"

She nodded her head slightly to show her compliance, and within a few minutes she was pushed up to a sitting position, pillows behind her, arms stretched out in an uncomfortable "V."

He seated himself beside her on the edge of the bed and placed the tray in her lap. She looked down at the food, but all she could think about was the coffee. He saw her interest in the cup and slipped a straw into it before raising it to her mouth. She sucked in the hot liquid too quickly, burning her tongue and making her cough. He put orange juice to her lips at an awkward angle, and it dribbled down her chin. He then spoon-fed her runny scrambled eggs and dry toast. When she finished, he removed the tray and situated her to restrain her legs again. She watched his every move.

He was a large man, tall. Wearing a white thermal shirt that outlined broad shoulders, a barrel chest, and thick muscular arms. He had on blue jeans, and she imagined that if she had met him in any other circumstances, she'd have considered him quite good-looking.

His curly black hair was tied back into a ponytail with meticulously kept sideburns. Deep-set brown eyes that were so dark she couldn't tell where the pupil ended and the retina started. Square jaw, prominent nose with thick eyebrows and lashes—she thought he looked middle-eastern perhaps. And then it crept back in—the foggy memory of being carried from her poolside. There was a flash: a quick and clear picture of his face and what had happened.

"Oh my God. You killed Trixie. *You killed my Trixie.*"

He didn't respond. He just continued what he was doing without looking up. With no real obvious reaction to what he had just been accused of.

"You filthy, heartless bastard. I am going to love to see you get what you deserve."

He finished securing her legs, retrieved the tray, and left the room without a word. When the door closed, she waited to hear him walk away. He lingered just outside for a few minutes before she heard his steps across the wooden floor.

After he had gone, Allison finally gave into the emotions she had been avoiding all morning and cried. She cried from frustration, fear, and rage. She sobbed for her innocent dog. She wept until she was exhausted and slipped back off to sleep until he entered the room again.

It was darker when she opened her eyes, and she was startled as he flipped on the lights. Again, he came in carrying a tray. He repeated the same process he had performed earlier until she was in an upright position with the tray in her lap.

She felt sick. The smell of the food repelled her. It was an unfamiliar dish of rice and fish in a thick broth that she could only stomach a few bites of, being solely interested in the water and hot tea. She still felt as if a hazy shroud covered her eyes, like an in-between dream state, and she was completely exhausted. Assuming it was the residual effects of whatever he had given her to knock her out, all she wanted to do was go back to sleep in hopes of waking up at home in her own bed with Trixie at her feet.

After allowing her to use the bedpan, he again secured her but left her uncovered and left her alone. She fell into instant slumber.

The next time she woke, it was to the sound of water running. There was a small lamp on next to her, and the light was on in the bathroom. Her covers were still off, and it was cold. She felt wet. Her inner thighs and bottom felt as if she were sitting in something damp and gooey.

She watched as he came out of the bathroom carrying a large silver bowl but didn't understand what was going on.

After setting the bowl on the floor beside the bed, he unhooked one of her legs. He acknowledged her awake but didn't offer any explanation.

"What are you doing?" she asked.

It came out sounding more fearful than she had anticipated. She couldn't think of any reason he would be focused on the lower part of her body and carrying a bowl of water except for one, and she wasn't awake enough to wrap her head around it or even protest. By that time her shoulders were absolutely killing her from her arms being above her head for so long, and her body was shivering. He lifted her free knee to the open and upright position.

"Lift up your ass."

His request didn't register at first. She laid there without moving.

He looked at her seriously and more than a little put-out. The look he gave her was enough to coax her into compliance, and she did as she was told.

He placed the bedpan under her, moved the bowl onto the bed, and started washing her. She tried to act as if it didn't bother her. There was a complete stranger between her legs, with no explanation or permission. And yet, she just laid there and watched. She knew fighting it wouldn't do her any good.

He spread her, rubbing the warm rag in all of her female parts, and she felt a bit uncomfortable in the fact that anger was the last thing it aroused in her.

When he dipped the rag back into the bowl, the water turned light pink, and she understood. She had started her period. She felt her face flush and directed her eyes to the ceiling. Not sure of why she was embarrassed. She had no reason to be; she couldn't control when her cycle started. But still, she was.

While trying to focus on anything but what he was doing, she felt him. His hands, the warmth of the rag, the way each touch was direct but gentle. As if he were exploring her, not missing one inch. She felt herself swelling, accompanied by the inner tingle that only came with being turned on. There was no use trying to suppress it.

She started to watch him, and when he returned her gaze, it made it much worse. She closed her eyes and bit her bottom lip. Her body started rhythmically moving without her consent, and her ears started to ring. She tried to stifle a moan with no success. She shifted her mind and focused on how much she hated him, but it was too late. It felt too good to ignore, and in an instant, her body gave in. She was wracked with the sweet explosion that spread through her groin and ended at the crown of her head and tips of her fingers and toes.

She lay panting for a moment, trying to recover. Not looking at him. Not sure if he was even aware that he had given her the first orgasm she'd had in years.

She heard him rip a package open and then felt him shove his finger into her vagina. The aftershocks of the orgasm made her ultra-sensitive; she squirmed and shuddered. Goosebumps covered her. Her brain was trying to make sense of what was happening and what had just happened. She realized that he was inserting a tampon.

Breath still ragged, she watched him as he removed the bowl, stripped the sheet out from under her, and replaced it with a thick towel.

He replaced the covers and looked down at her when he was finished. He seemed to be smirking. As if amused at what had taken place, and it infuriated her. After emptying the bowl and cleaning up in the bathroom, he gathered up the sheet and went to leave the room. As he got to the door, he turned and said,

"I am going to leave your leg free for now, for obvious reasons."

Cold, serious, and to the point.

But Allison could see the protruding lump in the front of his pants, and it gave her an odd satisfaction. When he left, she put aside the anger and shame long enough to smile to herself.

***

Leo stood outside of the door for a moment, holding the sheet, leaning against the door, his hand still on the doorknob.

He looked down at his obvious erection and got flustered. Like it wasn't part of him, as if his dick was a completely separate entity, he scolded it under his breath.

"Really? Are you freaking kidding me? What are we, fifteen?"

He let loose of the doorknob and headed to the kitchen to wash the bloody sheets. After dropping them into a boiling pot of water and soap, he made himself a cup of tea and sat down at the kitchen table. His mind wouldn't stop going over what had just taken place.

Her body, in all of its beauty, responded to his touch to such a mind-boggling degree. He had been with his fair share of women; that one in particular shouldn't have had the effect she had on him, especially since she was an unwilling participant.

He leaned back and adjusted himself. He had to get his mind off of it.

"Jesus, Leo. What in the hell is wrong with you?"

He hastily put on his jacket and went out to restock the firewood, hoping physical labor would redirect his thoughts.

After stacking the wood, he rinsed the sheets and went out into the dark to hang them out to dry, then went in for a bite of dinner.

He sat picking at his plate of food and eventually pushed it away, settling on a cup of black coffee.

He couldn't stop thinking about earlier. He envisioned her lying back, skin flushed, eyes dilated, gyrating her hips against his hand. It was a certain type of intoxication, and he was obsessing over it.

In that half hour, she had somehow become different. Not just a means to an end anymore, but a gorgeous woman that he wanted to claim. He kept fantasizing about what it would feel like to have her, and it was making him a bit crazy.

In four hours, he was going to have to repeat the process, and as much as he was looking forward to it, he knew it couldn't go on like that. In a little less than two weeks, she would be dead, and he would likely be in another country. Something he kept repeating over and over to himself.

He made a pallet on the floor in front of the fire and lay awake, staring at the ceiling. He knew he was not going to be able to sleep. Just after midnight, he went back in to check on her.

He turned on the hall light and left the door ajar. It illuminated her perfectly, and he stood over her, watching her sleep. Carefully peeling back the covers, he peered in to see if the towel had signs of blood on it. When he saw a dribble of red on the string, he went to fill the basin with water.

The second time, he tried to be more businesslike. Curbing his urge to be gentle and going about it in more of a methodical way. But after a few moments, he could feel her staring at him. He looked up at her, but her eyes were in the shadows, and all he could make out were the whites of them. He could see no expression or reaction. He could feel her rigid and resolved and knew there wouldn't be a repeat of earlier in the day. When he slipped in the tampon, he heard her gasp, again filling him with an unreasonable amount of excitement.

It left him oddly aggravated, and out of frustration, he finished as quickly as he could and left her, this time leaving the door open so as to get warmth from the living room fireplace.

He tried again to settle in for the night but gave up a few hours in and instead focused on a way out of having to tend to her personal hygiene needs for the next week.

He put on his shoes and coat, grabbed a flashlight, and went out to the shed. He was looking for a chain he remembered seeing months before. After moving a few things around, he located it, and inside an old rusty toolbox he found a padlock with the key still in it. He gathered them both up and brought them into the house. He cleaned the lock and made sure it worked, and he laid them out on the table for the morning. It looked like a solution to his problem.

He stoked the fire, and after putting on two extra logs, he returned to his bedroll and was finally able to go to sleep.

Four

She was startled, and her body jumped. She couldn't fathom a more irritating way to wake up. He was standing inside the bathroom door doing something *loudly*.

She watched as he unscrewed each hinge screw by hand and then pulled on the door. It didn't budge. He retrieved a hammer from the other room and spent a considerable amount of time banging on the doorframe with no result. Finally, he slipped a screwdriver into the hinge and applied pressure until it popped off. After repeating the process with the top one, the door let loose and leaned in against him. He carried it out of the room and then repeated the process with the bedroom door.

Why he had removed both doors, she had absolutely no idea.

He left the room and returned with a length of chain. At that point, she was a little more than curious. She lay glaring at him. Wasn't she incapacitated enough?

Without a word, he began unhooking her legs. He left her left ankle cuff on, and she could tell he was contemplating something. Chain in one hand, her foot in the other. After a pause in activity, he had it figured out, and shortly after, the heavy chain was attached to her ankle. It went around and through the iron footboard and was held in place with a padlock from his pocket.

After he was satisfied she was secure, he did something else she didn't see coming. He released her wrists.

She wasn't sure how to react. Initially too afraid to move, she still laid with her hands above her head. The relief was unbelievable. She didn't realize how much strain had been on her shoulders and forearms until she was loose. She didn't trust the unexpected sliver of freedom.

"You can move. The chain is long enough to reach the bathroom. Everything you should need is there. I won't remind you of what a bad idea it would be for you to step out of line."

After he left the room, Allison pulled her arms down to her chest and rubbed her wrists. Shocked at how quickly she'd adapted to the leather cuffs and how truly naked and bare she felt to suddenly be without them. She rubbed each one for a minute before sitting up and adjusting the shirt she was wearing to cover her crotch. She swung her legs over the side of the bed, the chain making a loud clanking as it slid all at once down the mattress and landed with a succession of thumps into a pile on the floor. It was ridiculously loud.

The opening to the bathroom was just opposite of the bed, and she made the few steps to the toilet, dragging the chain behind her. She sat on the cold toilet seat with her eyes closed for a few moments, silently rejoicing in the fact she didn't have to use the bedpan. Thank God for small favors.

Looking around the new space, she saw a bathtub and a boarded-up window, but nothing that would offer an escape. She did what she needed to do and washed her hands, standing over the bathroom sink, letting the steam rise before splashing the warm water on her face.

When she came out, there were clean sheets and her black undies and bra lying on the bed. Along with a towel, a washcloth, a bar of soap, and a pair of socks.

She stared at them.

"What is this, a fucking joke?" she said. How in the hell was she even supposed to get the underwear on? "Jerk."

She threw the pile onto the floor and laid back on the bed. Her head was swimming. She needed her medications.

He came back into the room, set the tray on the nightstand, and left. She didn't want food;

she needed a drink. She rolled up in the blanket, tucked her arms inside, and fell back asleep until he brought in the lunch tray. Again, she rolled over, got up long enough to go to the bathroom, and went back to bed.

By dinnertime, she had started to shake. Her stomach was cramping, and she was covered in sweat. Periodically breaking out in cold chills.

Leo took one look at her and knew immediately what was wrong; she was starting withdrawal.

He had seen his older brother go through it many times before addiction finally killed him, and he had not one ounce of sympathy for her. Alcohol and narcotics are choices, not illnesses. Each individual chooses to live that lifestyle, and each individual deserves what they endure because of it. It was going to get a whole lot worse before it got better, and he was relieved that he had changed her custody arrangements.

He left the food on the nightstand, brought in

an extra quilt, and left her alone to suffer through it.

The next morning, he woke to the sounds of her retching. Though he didn't feel guilt, he did have a fair amount of aggravation at the knowledge it was going to make things much more complicated over the next few days. It was going to be a long week.

He got up and put the kettle on, and knowing she wouldn't be able to eat breakfast, he skipped the hassle altogether. When the tea was done, he went in to take it to her.

The room smelled of vomit, and she was still positioned on her knees in front of the toilet. He put the clean sheet on the bed, then stood at the entrance to the bathroom watching her.

"I left green tea with ginger. It will help your stomach settle."

"Fuck off, asshole." She told him as a new vomiting spell took over.

"Suit yourself." He said as he left the room.

Shortly thereafter, he heard the bathtub filling with water. He took his tea onto the patio and sat outside to drink it. When he came back in, he could hear her crying. Still, he felt no remorse. Her consequences were her problem. Keeping her alive until it was safe to dump her and the car was his was his primary concern.

She was in the bath long enough to warrant attention, and he went to check on her.

Again, he stood at the entrance.

She lay in the bathtub, her ankle perched up on the edge with the chain half submerged, causing water to drip down onto the floor.

As if feeling his presence, she turned her head slightly to look at him. Her eyes were swollen and red, and when she saw him, she rolled them and closed them again. And then she spoke.

"I need my Xanax, or surely you have alcohol in this fucking hellhole."

"Lady, even if I had it, I wouldn't give it to you. This isn't a goddamn Holiday Inn."

He spun on his heels and quickly left the room. Anger was rising in him for no apparent reason other than the fact she treated him as if he were a servant. Talking down to him seemed to give her pleasure.

"Neurotic bitch." He said under his breath as he walked outside.

The air was frigid, and he watched as his breath made clouds out in front of him with each exhale. He lit a cigarette to calm his nerves.

She rubbed him the wrong way in every way.

He had underestimated just how much of an annoyance having her under the same roof would be. Or maybe the aggravation had been created in the last twenty-four hours.

No matter; using her words as an attempted power play would not rescue her from her inevitable fate. He stood on the porch long enough to calm down. He finished his cigarette and went back in to make food.

****

She spent the next three days either hovering over the toilet or on it. At night she laid in her own sweat and screamed out from what he could only guess were nightmares or severe body spasms. Her body shook and shivered no matter how warm it was or how many blankets she had on her.

The only thing he saw her consume was water, with the exception of twice when she drank warm apple cider. He assumed it was because it was the only thing she could assimilate with alcohol.

He brought her a tray for breakfast, lunch, and dinner. Each one either sat untouched or ended up thrown against a wall. There was a rage inside of her that, had she had the energy to do something about, he knew she would.

Her mouth became fouler with each day, and when she did sleep, it was from pure exhaustion. She was making it easy to dislike her.

And then, on her sixth day of captivity, a calmness set in. The tremors seemed to subside, and her skin took on some color. There was no longer sweat running down her throat, and her eyes ceased to bulge. He thought the worst must be over.

The next morning, he made her breakfast tray and slipped into the room before daybreak. As he turned to leave, he heard the chain hit the floor with a loud thump, and before he knew what was happening, she was on him.

She jumped on his back and hit him with her fists. Her legs twisted tightly around his waist; the weight of the chain was heavy against his thigh, side, and shin, and she had a fistful of his hair.

She was half his size, and after the initial shock, he flicked her off of him easily enough. She landed on the ground with a thud, and that's where she stayed. He stood over her, tense and waiting for her to attack again, but there she lay, on the floor, completely still.

He saw from under her blond hair a line of dark, thick blood seeping down her neck. He leaned over to get a better look. Apprehensively, he squatted down and tilted her head to the side. There was a gash just behind her ear.

He looked around, trying to make sense of it. She must have hit it on the nightstand.

Not knowing what to do, adrenaline coursed through his veins and caused him to shake, and he couldn't form a clear plan. He left the room long enough to grab a washcloth and a towel and came back to clean up the wound. Not sure what else to do, he applied pressure to the area until the bleeding stopped and wrapped her head in the towel. While moving her to the bed, she moaned, and he knew she was going to be okay.

Not wanting a repeat, he secured her left wrist to its original position, cleaned up the floor, and left her again. She had more spunk than he gave her credit for, and for some reason he found it funny.

Those last few days of withdrawal had irrationally caused her to misplace her fear. He laughed out loud as he made his way to the living room. What a crazy bitch.

Five

Ben sat in the waiting room of the police station, looking around. He hadn't slept more than a few hours since he found out his mother was gone. No matter how many times he went over it in his mind, it just made no sense. He was more than concerned; he was lost. She had been his best friend since he was a teenager, and he felt her absence more than anyone. Especially since there hadn't been a request for ransom or a clue as to why someone would have taken her to begin with.

Consumed in his thoughts, he didn't notice when Jake and his father emerged from the elevator.

"I had a hell of a time finding a parking space; we are four blocks away." Jake said, snapping him back to the present.

Ben looked past him at Heath. He hadn't expected to see him there and raised his eyebrows as if asking for an explanation.

"Ben." Heath said, with a slight nod, foregoing any forced signs of fatherly affection.

"Dad." He said, waiting for him to explain.

"They called me this afternoon. Said they had more questions." He looked down and grabbed the back of his neck, running his fingers into his shirt collar and around to the front as if it were choking him. His tie was already loose and resting midway down his chest, and he started unbuttoning the top three buttons in succession. It appeared that he had already had his afternoon scotch. There was no mistaking that look. Beads of sweat were trickling down his sideburns; his nervousness was palpable.

Ben was disgusted. Even more than normal. Something he didn't know was possible until he felt it.

It was more than the years of disagreements or harsh opinions about his lifestyle that his father had no problem voicing whenever he got the chance. It was Ben's complete loss of respect and the absence of what should have come naturally. He felt no love for the man. He never had. And as far as he could tell, his father felt the same way. The only thing he had ever received from him was consistent proof in every way that he was his biggest disappointment. As far as Ben was concerned, it was mutual.

Heath was an absent parent. Always out of town or at the office when anything required his attendance. He had not been present for one doctor's appointment or baseball game, and Ben couldn't remember him being around for any significant milestone in his life. Even missing his graduation from high school, university, and later culinary school. He proved in every way possible that he simply didn't care.

Just as his father took a seat, a man came from an office next to the waiting area. He approached Ben, extending his hand.

"I'm detective Shultz; my partner, detective Williams, is running late and will join us shortly."

He shook each of their hands, and after instructing Heath and Jake to stay in the waiting room, he headed back into the office with Ben following close behind.

Once inside, he had a seat on the far side of a table and opened a file he had brought in under his arm. Ben sat opposite him and scooted the chair closer, positioning his arms out and clasping his hands together. He waited while the officer seemed to scan a few pages.

When he finally looked up, he still seemed to be preoccupied.

"So, Mr. Parker, I am going to ask you a few questions, on the record. I am obligated to tell you that you don't have to be here, and you don't have to participate in this interview. If you feel you need an attorney present, I can wait until you have counsel. It is your right, and it is entirely up to you."

Ben answered,

"You can call me Ben, and do I need one?"

"I can't answer that. It is your choice."

The detective paused, hunched over the paperwork, and stared, waiting for his answer. He displayed no signs of aggression, and it gave Ben a false sense of ease.

"I don't mind answering any questions you have. I'll do anything I can to help find my mother. But I'm not sure what I can add to what I have already told the other detective."

Shultz looked like every single cop he had ever seen on television. Sleep deprived and put out. Something in his mannerism screamed distrust even if his words said otherwise. His shirt was pressed and starched, his nails manicured, but his skin had a sheen that only comes from a diet of greasy burgers and diner fare, and he smelled of stale cigarette smoke. He was probably in his forties, but with his obvious cynicism and the dark bags under his eyes, he could have been older.

"Can I get you something to drink? Coffee? Water?"

Just as he asked the question, the door

opened and the other detective stepped in. It was the same guy who had interviewed him in his living room a few days prior. Ben didn't bother rising; he remained seated and shook his hand from where he was. He declined the offer for a beverage, just wanting to get the interview over with.

Officer Williams pulled a chair from the corner and was seated at the end of the table, creating a triangle between the men. Ben wasn't sure why the new arrangement made him feel uncomfortable; he only knew it did. He shifted in his seat.

Shultz spoke again.

"I know you have already answered many of these questions, but bear with me. We need to get a complete picture."

Ben nodded.

"When was the last time you saw your mother?"

"The night of her birthday party."

"I'm going to need you to be more specific. Please answer the question as if it is the first time you've been asked."

"Okay. Last Thursday night."

"At what time?"

"After the dinner party. I was the last to

leave. It was almost eleven.”

“And what was your mother doing when you left?”

“She was getting ready to go to bed, as far as I know.”

“Was she drunk?”

Ben tried to suppress a chuckle.

“It was her birthday, and it was late. I mean, she wasn’t any more drunk than she always gets at those functions. I don’t know, more drunk than some, less drunk than others.”

“I see. And does she always drink to excess?”

Ben felt as if he was betraying her in an odd way by telling the truth. But he did anyway.

“Yeah, she and Dad both do.”

“Okay, Benjamin. I want you to think back to the dinner party. Do you remember seeing anything unusual? Anyone that seemed to have an issue or problem with her, or angry words exchanged?”

“No, not at all. Things went smoothly. But I was in the kitchen a lot of the time. My company handled the party.”

“Was your father there when you left?”

Ben broke eye contact and looked at the smooth surface of the table for a moment, fidgeting with his hands.

"I don't know. I didn't see him. I assumed he was already upstairs, but I can't say whether he was or wasn't, to be honest."

Shultz leaned back a bit. Years of doing his job enabled him to hear what wasn't being said. After exchanging a quick glance with the other officer, he continued.

"How would you describe your parents' relationship?"

Ben sighed deeply and sat back in his chair. He had never once in his life felt the need to protect his father, and that day was no different.

"Relationship is a stretch. They are two people who live in the same house but do everything in their power not to occupy the same space. They coexist, nothing more. But if you are asking me if they fight, no, they don't."

Neither detective deviated their focus from him, not asking another question but wanting more of an answer to the previous one.

"Look, Mom and Dad have their issues. I'm being honest when I say Mom keeps most of that private. The only thing I do know for sure is that Dad has affairs. He has for years. Mom just accepted it at some point and focuses on her own life."

That response caused detective Williams to lean forward and start his own line of questioning.

"So, you are saying that she *knew* your father was stepping out and it didn't *bother her*?"

"If it bothered her, I didn't know about it. And if anyone would have known, it would have been me."

Williams shot off the next question.

"And did your mother ever have extramarital affairs?"

"Not that I know of."

Shultz was looking at notes in front of him and, without looking up, asked,

"How's your catering business doing, Ben?"

"It is doing well. We took a hit during the pandemic, but things are picking up quickly. I have no reason to be concerned, and in fact, I feel pretty optimistic."

"Do you lean on your parents for financial support at all?"

That question felt accusatory, causing Ben to sit up straighter before he answered.

"No. When my grandfather died, he left me enough money to start my business and sustain me while I got it off the ground. I have not needed to ask my parents for money. Not since college."

Williams,

"And your partner?"

Ben's whole body went rigid.

"What about him?"

"From what I understand, your father said Jake and your mother are close. He's treated like a second son, and yet he was absent for her birthday dinner party. I find that peculiar. And from what I can see, he isn't exactly making waves with his art. He's far from successful. So would he have been secretly dependent on money from her?"

"Jake does okay. He couldn't come that night because he had an exhibit the following Saturday and had to work. But I assure you, we manage just fine. If he needed money, he would have asked me, not mom."

He felt immediately protective of Jake. His answer came out angrier than he had intended, and he didn't feel sorry about it.

Shultz took his glasses off, rubbing his fingers across his forehead and the bridge of his nose before putting them back on and showing a complete change in his demeanor. He became harsh and direct.

"Benjamin, are you aware that you are the beneficiary on all of your mother's life insurance? As well as the sole heir of her estate."

Ben felt as if a bucket of hot water had just

been dumped over his head. He felt himself flush; his ears began to ring, and the room spun. In that instant, he understood the purpose of the interview.

"What?" is all he could say.

Williams perked up and adjusted his chair, pulling it closer to Ben, preventing him from properly digesting what he had just been told.

"Are you surprised? *Surely not. Surely,* as close as you are to your mother, you know that she is leaving everything to you? If anything happens to her, you will inherit every dime of her twelve million as well as her life insurance."

Ben was speechless. He sat repeating in his mind what the detective had just said. Lingering over the "twelve million" again and again. Trying to make sense of it, until he heard himself say it out loud.

"Twelve million. *Twelve million?*"

Williams was on his feet, shoving the chair out of the way with such force it teetered and screeched as it slid across the linoleum.

"Benjamin, you do not expect us to believe that *this is NEWS TO YOU! That you had no idea?* After just now telling us how close you are to your mother!"

He had one hand on his hip; the other he was using to accentuate his words. Running it about in the air, as if he were on a stage. He came back and sat on the edge of the chair, facing Ben with his elbows on his knees. Looking him straight in the eyes. He adjusted his tone and again repeated his accusation.

"She's gone; her car is gone, but nothing else of value was taken. There have been no attempts at contact for ransom. You said yourself there was no inner turmoil in her marriage and no outside influences.

In your own words, you described her as well-adjusted and content, which means she wouldn't have run off on her own. The only clue we have is the dead family pet. Which tells us it was something personal against your mother *and* your father since he was so torn up over it. In all my years doing this job, I've never seen a grown man so upset over an animal. Her abduction had to be an inside job, and you are the only one who would benefit from all of this.   So, I want you to think again. This time *harder*. Who would want your mother enough to risk abducting her from her own house with the added risk of fleeing in *her* car?"

Ben sat. His hands had repositioned at some point and were resting inside his knees. He stared at them, unable to think of anything except their mention of twelve million dollars. He really had no idea that she had that much money. He knew that his grandparents had left her well-off, but it never occurred to him that she was a millionaire.

Thinking back over the last five years, nothing had changed. She still lived in the same house, and although she had recently upgraded her Audi, her life was far from extravagant. He couldn't even remember the last time she'd taken a trip or gone on a vacation. There was absolutely no proof that she was that wealthy. Hell, he didn't know his grandparents were that wealthy. They too had lived modestly. He was lost in his own thoughts over the matter and couldn't bring forth a reasonable response—any response. He just shook his head back and forth and stared at the detective, mute.

Williams showed his frustration by sitting up and sweeping his arms out in disbelief. He exhaled and looked at Shultz.

When Ben finally found his voice, it was to say that he had changed his mind.

"In light of things, I think it would be better for me to consult an attorney."

He then got up, extended his hand to each of the detectives, and turned to exit the room.

Shultz thanked him for his time and followed him to the door. As Ben turned the knob, he paused and looked back. Choosing to direct his words to Shultz instead of Williams.

"You know, I feel it's important to let you know that my father despised Trixie. He had an unreasonable dislike for her from the second we got her."

As Ben opened the door, he stopped one last time and, lowering his voice, said,

"I've never seen him hate another dog; just her."

He stood silent for a moment, adding weight to his last words.

"I'd appreciate being kept in the loop on this investigation. My mother is alive, and whether you believe it or not, I more than anyone want her found."

He walked out without waiting for a response from either of them.

Once Ben was far enough from earshot, both detectives were more than a little confused and stood staring at each other. The new piece of information was a proverbial bombshell.

Six

Ben and Jake walked in silence to the car. Jake was still in the dark about why they'd left in such a hurry and why he hadn't been interviewed.

When they were safely buckled in, Jake went to pull out of the place he'd had to parallel park in, but not before turning to Ben and asking him what was going on.

Ben sat, staring ahead. There was something so unsettling about the whole situation, made worse by the detectives' statements about his father's response to Trixie. It had started a nagging in his mind and a feeling deep in the pit of his stomach he couldn't shake. He started to accept what he was thinking as more than a suspicion before he considered verbalizing it to Jake.

"Honey, are you hungry?"

Jake was busy consulting his traffic app but paused long enough to answer.

"I could eat, and it would save us from getting onto the busy interstate during rush hour."

"I'll tell you all about it over dinner."

A few minutes later, they were seated in a downtown sandwich shop, sipping iced tea and waiting on their order. The ceiling fan closest to them off-kilter just enough to lend an annoying, consistent thump to the space.

Jake sat observing Ben. Years of being together had taught him not to pressure Ben for an answer; he would get it out once he had over-analyzed the subject enough to put it into words. That day being no different except that what he had to say came quicker than he expected.

"Jake, did you ever see dad interact with Trixie?"

Jake didn't hesitate. He sat back in the booth, tilted his head up, and let out a short laugh.

"No, never. He hated that dog. Why?"

Ben didn't join him in seeing the humor but mirrored his partner and sat back in the booth.

"Detective Williams said that dad was extremely upset over Trixie's death. Unusually so. He said that he had never seen a man get so emotional over a pet."

"What? That is strange, but what does that have to do with anything?"

And then he understood.

"Oh! *ohhhh.* Babe, you can't think what I

think you're thinking. Come on now! Your father is the most passive person I know! No way!"

Ben looked out the window as he told Jake,

"But my father defends the worst of the worst, criminals who are used to solving problems in unorthodox ways."

"I am unaware of what problem you are referring to, Ben."

"That's what I'm trying to figure out. And there's more."

Jake sat forward, eager to hear whatever it was that had Ben acting so odd.

"Apparently, my mother is a millionaire. If anything happens to her, I am the sole heir to twelve million dollars."

Ben was still staring out the window when he delivered the news, turning his head in time to see Jake's posture change to upright and rigid before spreading his arms open, positioning his elbows on the back of his seat, and resting against it. His mouth was half open, his eyebrows were drawn together, and his gaze was serious and piercing. He had definitely heard his words, but Ben could see his mind scrambling for a correct response. He sat there silent. The truth is that there was no correct way to respond.

It took a few minutes for the shock to wear off enough for him to speak.

"Jesus Christ, Ben. That's a lot of money. And from what I gather, a good motive."

Out of the two of them, Ben was the overthinker, and Jake was the passionate one. It only took a few minutes for him to understand what Ben was still trying to wrap his head around.

Ben continued speaking. More to hear out loud what he was hashing out in his mind than for Jake's input.

"Yeah. I am the beneficiary of her life insurance policy as well. Which makes it all the more confusing as to why Dad would be acting out of character."

"And why hasn't there been a ransom demand? You and I both know Trixie's death was probably like Christmas for him, so why would he act otherwise? And why would he have mom taken if he wouldn't stand to gain from it? Unless he didn't know he wasn't the beneficiary, and I don't know how that would be possible."

Jake leaned all the way forward and started to say something when the waitress came with their food.

They waited until both plates were in front of them and tea glasses refilled, never taking their eyes off of one another.

When she was gone, again Jake leaned in. He

whispered as if it would matter if someone else heard.

"Come on. I know you and your father have your issues, but you surely cannot believe he is behind this. Why would he? He does well for himself, and being married to your mother, wouldn't he have access to those funds anyway? And babe, I have more than a few doubts that he could even orchestrate something of this magnitude."

Ben replied,

"I don't know. I only know that I have a feeling. A feeling I can't ignore."

Jake paused long enough to pour ketchup all over his fries, and after salting them and popping one in his mouth, he again leaned over his dinner and said,

"Ben. Think about what you are saying. If you believe this, the only way this would pan out for your father is for your mother to be dead. If he in fact was behind this, that means that he has the intention of killing her. And that is *if* he believes he is the beneficiary. If he finds out otherwise, that means you are in danger. So, the real question is, do you think your father could kill not just your mother but whoever stands in his way? *Do you believe your father is a murderer*? Kidnapping is a far cry from killing someone. Seems like something you should be pretty damn sure about before you go accusing."

Ben shoved his plate aside, his appetite gone. Mainly because the answer to Jake's question was yes. He had no problem completely believing his father was capable of whatever it took to satiate his greed. He grew up around the man; nothing was ever enough for him. To include his home, investments, and women. He couldn't count how many times as a kid he and his mother had argued over his father's extravagance. He was always trying to live beyond their means. His father had no shame when it came to getting ahead. His profession proved that. And if he and his mother were casualties in his personal war, it would be no love lost.

He got a shiver down his spine, then suddenly, a wave of fear. For the first time in his life, he felt unsafe. It told him everything he needed to know. His sixth sense had him on high alert. He knew he needed to find out why.

He looked around the restaurant before digging into his pocket for cash, throwing it on the table and beckoning Jake.

"Let's go."

More than a little aggravated, Jake followed him out of the restaurant, carrying half of his sandwich.

***

Monique knew there was something wrong from the second they met that afternoon. They barely made it into the seedy motel room before Heath attacked her. Almost ferocious in his actions, lustful and angry. He hadn't even bothered getting undressed, raising her dress and forcing himself inside of her right inside the door.

He released his pent-up frustration with such aggression; she didn't have time to react. Each pump shoved her against the hard wall, raking her shoulders and back on the rough texture. With no eye contact or concern. She endured him and was grateful when it was over.

He lingered a few moments afterward, still inside of her, panting and shaky before abruptly pulling out and letting go of her hips. She stumbled and slid down the wall to her knees.

He left her there, lighting a cigarette on his way to the bed.

She sat crumpled on the floor, trying to hold back tears, but they were persistent, and she lost the battle.

Crying was a weakness, and after she allowed it to play out, she

wiped her nose on the back of her arm, collected herself, and stood.

Legs wobbly, anger soon replaced her hurt feelings, and without thinking, she started screaming profanity at him in French while simultaneously pulling her skirt down and trying to unlock the door to leave.

Just as the door broke loose, she felt his arm come across her shoulder from behind. Heath slammed it closed again and, as if suddenly returning to himself, buried his head in the back of her neck.

They stood at the door for a moment, he leaning against her.

"I am sorry. Please forgive me, my love. I am so sorry. I shouldn't have acted that way. Please don't go. Please."

His arms moved down around her waist, and all of the anger and aggression he had displayed earlier was replaced with gentle touches and tender words of apology. Until her anger melted away.

He softly pulled on her, leading her away from the door and to the bed, where he cradled her in his arms. Running his hands through her hair and peppering the top of her head with kisses.

"My darling, will you ever forgive me?"

She was no longer angry and rejoiced in his drastic change in demeanor. And before her eyes were even dry, she was smiling. Receiving his kisses and his apology wholeheartedly.

"Yes, I forgive you. But you must tell me what happened. I don't understand why we must be in this awful place, and why must we be so careful now? When will it be over? How long must I be the secret? You promised this would be over soon. I don't know what to believe anymore. Make it make sense to me before I lose my mind."

Their positions had changed during her speech, and then it was he who laid with his head on her chest while she rubbed his hair. Her thick French accent vibrating in his ear and giving him the first bit of calm he had experienced in days. He closed his eyes and tried to think through the onslaught of new information he had received that day before finally settling on the proper words to explain.

"I told you why we have to change our meeting arrangements; I don't mind the other girls from my past being interviewed; they truly do not know a thing. But you are a different story. The only way to protect you is to take you out of the mix altogether. It won't be much longer, and we will be back at the Ritz Carlton."

He paused before delivering the next blow.

"My wife is smarter than I gave her credit for, my dear."

She didn't give him time to finish before sitting up so she could look at him as he spoke.

"Why do you say that?"

There was a hint of suspicion in her voice. Although young, she was no fool and had trouble not being suspicious of his every word the last six months. Being a beautiful girl in a foreign country had given her insight into American men. Especially the older ones who promised her the world. They all had a problem with delivering. She waited for what she perceived as his excuse.

"It seems that she has named Ben as her heir. As well as the beneficiary on all life insurance."

She tried to contain herself and put on an understanding facade, but inside she was boiling. She looked down at him, waiting for him to continue. Hoping he would say something to contradict what he had just revealed to her.

"What does this mean?"

"It means that they have zeroed in on Ben as the one behind her abduction, which is perfect. But it also means that I will not benefit from her death. Except for the small policy I took out on her some years back, which is peanuts compared to what she is worth."

His voice trailed off. He had already thought

of every aspect of what was happening; it had consumed him since he left the police station. But no matter how many times he tried to come up with a different solution, there was only one way out that he could see. He wasn't ready to accept that particular remedy yet.

Even though he and Ben were far from normal in the father-son department, he was still his son. He was the only living family member he had. More than that, Ben was the only person on the planet with whom he shared blood. He felt conflicted.

As much as he hated Allison before, there was no comparison to the contempt he felt for her after he found out all of his trouble was only going to serve in making his son a very wealthy man. A son who neither looked nor acted anything like him. A son who embodied every single detestable characteristic he could imagine. He was exactly like *her*—not him.

In one way or another, she was always ruining his life and making him miserable. He felt as if it was her personal vendetta to do so.

The position he was in was worse than before. Now that it was done, he would have to pay the mob for the money he owed them as well as for her kidnapping. His tab was growing larger. With no payout, he was in trouble.

Monique broke the silence.

"And what if your son had an accident?"

Her words shocked Heath. Always saying out loud what he barely allowed himself to think. As if she were swimming around in his head. He looked up at her.

"I suppose I would inherit by default. There isn't anyone else. Neither of us has family left or anyone to pass it down to, except for Benjamin."

They silently stared at one another for a minute before Monique relayed her wishes in the only way she knew how. She reached down and slid her hand down into his underwear, stroking him until he was hard enough. She removed her panties and climbed on top of him.

On her heels, hovering with the tip of him inside of her, she teased him. He grabbed her hips, trying to force himself further into her, but she resisted. She held the key, and he knew without her asking what she wanted to hear. She didn't move or do the thing that he loved. Instead, she withheld until he said what she wanted him to say.

It was her way; it was his way. They always got what they wanted from each other.

He bolted upright, grabbing her ponytail in one hand and her waist in the other as he rammed himself all of the way into her. She let out a short, sharp gasp.

He pulled her head over, and when his lips were touching her earlobe, he vocalized his intent.

"People have accidents all of the time."

She rewarded him with her rhythmic bounce.

And just like that, the solution was born and agreed upon.

Seven

After waking up with a massive headache and her left arm secured to the headboard again, Allison realized she was going to have to use her brain. She hadn't had the chance to form a clear plan in the last week due to her body's response to the lack of narcotics.

She lay on her left side in a fetal position, considering her options.

She knew from experience that there were two different approaches that worked with men. One was strength and force; the other was to be feminine and kind. She didn't have much experience with the second. But the first option wasn't doing anything but making the situation worse. So, she made up her mind to subdue her natural tendency for aggression and anger and replace it with the softest demeanor she could muster. She would figure out a way to gain his trust and find her way out. She would focus on escaping.

Wrapped up in her own thoughts, she didn't hear him come in. The air was frigid as night fell, and she had remained in bed all day without access to the toilet. She rolled over to face him. As he set the tray of food on the nightstand and turned on the lamp, she said in the gentlest way she knew how,

"I need to use the bathroom. I promise I won't do anything stupid again if you release my arm. I am sorry; I don't know what got into me."

She followed her request with,

"Please?"

Leo stood over her and immediately noted the change in her tone. He felt suspicious. But not enough to prevent his agreement. In minutes, she was free to move around the room again. He decided he would rather risk it than return to being her personal needs attendant.

She went to the bathroom and stood in front of the mirror. Her reflection was almost unrecognizable. Her skin was pale, her face gaunt, her lips chapped and peeling, and her right jaw a bit swollen. She reached around to the bump behind her ear. It was sore but crusted over; her hair was matted and tangled around it. Blood had trickled down her neck and left dark brown stains on the white cotton shirt she was wearing. She stripped it off and decided to run a bath. All the while he stood observing her from just outside the doorway. She knew it was not going to be easy to gain his trust. But what else did she have to do? Time was something she seemed to have a lot of recently.

She wasn't sure if the idea presented itself because she had formed a plan and it was fresh in her mind, or if it had been there all along and she had been too sick to see it.

While she lingered in the bath, enjoying the stillness and absorbing the heat from the water, her foot that was perched on the edge slid in. Being attached to a chain didn't prevent it, and in fact, once it started to sink, the weight of the ankle restraint propelled it quicker. She didn't fight it, allowing her foot to sink all the way to the bottom.

When the water became tepid, she leaned up to open the hot water valve and refresh the bath. As she leaned back into the water, she noticed the ankle cuff slid down a little. Down to the base of her heel. The leather was softening. She put her hand down, slipped her fingers under the band, and pulled. She knew immediately, with a little more time and work, it would become loose enough to slip off.

Feeling his gaze, she laid back, completely submerging herself. Soaking her hair and trying not to show her excitement at the discovery. When she emerged, from the corner of her eye, she saw him leave the bedroom.

Again, she checked the cuff, and there was no doubt that it was becoming pliable. She felt confident she could free herself from it.

Not wanting to let on, she finished her bath, dried off, and returned to the bed. Immediately putting on the clean shirt he had left for her and climbing under the cover to hide the cuff from his view.

There was a renewal in her. The revelation made her feel optimistic, and she was able to eat. She ate every bit of the strange dinner dish of lamb and rice and was surprised at how good it actually tasted. It was the first meal she'd wanted since being in captivity.

When she was finished, he collected the tray and brought in a pot of hot tea. That too, she drank. She emptied the pot, and he seemed pleased. Even asking her if she wanted anything more. Allison gave him the sweetest smile before declining his generous offer, then told him that she only wished for sleep.

He left her there for the evening, giving her all the time she needed to quietly pull and pry until she finagled the restraint all of the way over her foot.

It was almost too much for her to take.

She stayed then, willingly on the bed, not knowing what to do, completely free of restraints.

Unclear about her next move, she secretly

laid and savored her newfound freedom. Knowing that it was only a matter of time.

Those next few hours felt like a lifetime while she patiently waited for her chance. Knowing at some point he would go to sleep. She envisioned what was possibly beyond the four walls she had become accustomed to and wondered how close the nearest neighbor or business was. She thought of finding a highway and flagging someone down, and what a dramatic rescue it would be when she explained her recent days, even considering the news coverage and her captor's capture.

She smiled to herself as dozens of different scenarios played out in her mind.

She heard him in the other room. She listened as he did dishes and swept the floor. She patiently waited as he made trips outside and back in again, dropping loads of firewood onto the wooden floor. His Zippo lighter snapped closed, she smelled cigarette smoke, and then the light coming into her bedroom went dim. And still, she stayed in her bed.

When the house was completely quiet and she hadn't heard movement of any kind long enough to be sure, she made her move.

Slowly, she slipped out from under the covers and put both feet on the floor. It was much colder than she'd anticipated, and she sat for a bit considering her options. If it was that cold inside, it would be much worse outside. She looked around the room; the only thing she had at her disposal was her black robe and panties and a pair of socks. Quietly, she put them on, pausing periodically to listen for movement.

When she had them on, she crept up to the door and peered down the hallway. The only light was coming from the fireplace, casting shadows that flickered and moved. She held on to the wall as she took tiny, light steps, the old wooden floor creaking under her weight. Each step forward caused more anxiety than the last.

When she got to the end of the hallway, she stopped. It opened into a larger room, with an old overstuffed chair and table directly in front of her on the left and a small kitchen behind it. She didn't see him. She would have to step into the room blindly.

Cautiously, she bent her upper body forward, leaving her feet planted exactly where they were in the safety of the hallway. She scanned the area. The fireplace took up the wall to the right of the hall. Beyond that, there was the front wall of the cabin with a large window, and on the other side of the window was what she assumed was the front door. She never considered looking down until she saw something move.

There on the floor in front of the fireplace was

a sleeping bag, and she could see his dark hair poking out from it. She retreated to the safety of the hallway for a moment. Then she made her move.

Apprehensively, she tiptoed around him. Skirting in between the chair and his makeshift bed. Choosing her path as far away from him as she could. Her heart beating in her ears and all but holding her breath. Never considering what she would do if the door was locked. Hope and adrenaline propelled her forward.

He never moved, and by the time she made it to the door, she was filled with a new confidence, never turning back to look at him or the prison she was so close to escaping.

When the doorknob was finally in her hand, she didn't hesitate. And with no resistance or trouble, it turned, and the door opened. Even when it squeaked on its hinges, she didn't look back. Stepping over the threshold and onto the dimly lit porch, not taking the risk to close the door behind her.

Being acutely aware of her limited time, she took the steps by twos. Stumbling down the last and landing on all fours. She quickly recovered, jumped up, and without knowing her surroundings, ran aimlessly toward the tree line. She stepped on something sharp, and it cut through her sock and deep into her foot.

It only slowed her down; she didn't stop.

She reached the safety of the woods and paused. She turned around to get an overall picture of the open area she'd just crossed.

The small porch light loaned minimal aid. She stood with labored breathing and allowed her eyes to adjust.

There was a small building on one end, and on the other she spotted what looked to be two vehicles. A Jeep and a car. As her vision became clearer and she focused, she realized it was her very own Audi. She put aside the complete confusion for a minute to consider her options. But she couldn't help but wonder, how in the hell did he manage to have her car?

She was freezing. There were frozen dewdrops on the ground, and already, her hands and feet were beginning to feel numb and painful. She mentally scolded herself for not thinking it through and planning better.

While she stood, peering from behind a cedar tree, she saw the front door of the cabin open completely.   And then she saw his silhouette and knew he was awake and in pursuit.

***

Leo awoke to a cold breeze on his face. Instinctively, he knew something was amiss. He jumped up, saw the door ajar, and immediately ran to the bedroom and flipped on the light. The cuff and chain laid across an empty bed.

"That clever bitch."

Forgoing trying to find his pants, he quickly put on his boots and jacket and grabbed his flashlight on the way out the door. But once outside, he slowed his pace. Comfortable in the knowledge that not only were they miles away from anyone, but it was also below freezing. How far could she have gotten in a thin shirt and socked feet?

He stood at the top of the steps, surveying the area with no sign of her. Stepping off of the porch, he turned on his flashlight and pointed it in the direction of the vehicles, and then past them and down the drive. He started to walk toward the woodshed, but all of the clues told him to focus in another direction. On the frosty ground was a clear trail of frostless footprints and flattened grass. He followed it with the beam of light and saw that it led into a dense thicket. He spotted something dark and newly wet on a wide yellow leaf and crouched down to touch it. He rubbed it between his thumb and forefinger before bringing his hand closer to his face. He saw that it was blood. He wiped his fingers on his jacket and stood.

Not going any further, he decided to appeal

to her common sense instead of wasting both of their time.

"Listen, lady. We are at least a hundred miles away from anyone. There are no neighbors or main roads. There is nowhere to run. If you stay out, you will freeze to death by morning. Don't be stupid."

He waited a few moments and rephrased and repeated his words a bit louder with no response. The longer he stood out in the weather in his boxers, the angrier he got. Even though he couldn't see her, he felt her presence and knew she was there. He knew she heard him. Again, he spoke.

"I told you that I wasn't going to hurt you. Just come back, and we can forget this ever happened. I know you're injured; I see the blood. Just come out, and we can go in and take care of it."

She still didn't reply or come out, but he heard a branch snap. As if she had shifted her weight. He shone the flashlight in the direction of the sound but still couldn't see her. And then he heard a sniffle and spotted clouds coming from her warm breath.

After half an hour of pleading, he was getting pissed off. The next words that he spoke came from a place of anger and resentment.

"Hear this. You are safer with me in that cabin than you are anywhere else. I was hired to take you, and if this thing doesn't go as planned, you will end up dead anyway. Do you understand what I am saying?"

She answered.

"My husband will find me, and when he does, he will kill you!"

He was completely aggravated at that point, and without thinking, he blurted out with a sarcastic chuckle.

"*Your husband?* YOUR HUSBAND IS NOT COMING TO YOUR RESCUE! *WHO DO YOU THINK SET THIS ALL UP?* You seriously cannot be this ignorant."

"You are a liar; I don't *believe you.*" YOU'RE A GOD-DAMNED LIAR!"

There was fear and disbelief in her constricted words. She spoke like she had a hand around her throat. Shallow, as if trying desperately not to weep, and in that moment, he felt sorry for her.

Leo relaxed his shoulders and looked down. Softening his tone and manner before coming at her in a new way.

"Allison. That is your name, right? Allison? What I said is true. Think about it. How do you think I got your car? Why do you think you can't remember the night I brought you here? If I didn't drug you, think about who did. I promise if you give up, no harm will come to you. But out of my possession, you are in danger. You are safer here than anywhere right now, whether you believe me or not. I don't see that you have any other choice but to believe me."

That was his last try. He was cold, tired, and done with the game. He charged through the trees and caught her just as she tried to run.

He threw her over his shoulder and carried her, kicking and screaming, into the house.

Eight

With some difficulty, he brought her in, slamming the door closed behind him and throwing her onto the chair. Where she immediately jumped up and went full force back towards it. He quickly extended his arm in front of her before she even made it halfway. It had the same effect as clotheslining someone, and she bounced backwards and fell, landing on her bottom.

He bent down and, with one fluid movement, plucked her up from the ground and deposited her into the chair again. He stood over her, and as she propelled forward to try again, he pinned her shoulders to the back of the chair and spoke.

"I am about done with your shit. All of the years of drugs and alcohol must have damaged your brain. I promise you... you really do not want to fuck with me right now."

He was only a few inches from her face, and Allison could see he was serious. Enough that she stopped fighting and sat still.

"Your foot needs attention. Now fucking sit here, and allow me to get what I need to get to take care of it."

He didn't ease up on the pressure to her shoulders until she nodded in agreement.

He bent down and pulled the cold, wet sock from her foot. It was almost completely saturated in blood. He peeled it off slowly, and when he got it off, he pulled her leg up and rested it on his knee to take a look.

It was a bad cut, essentially leaving a two-inch gash along the soft middle of her foot. It was concerning. He was squatting down, making them eye level to one another and told her,

"This needs stitches. I will do what I can, but I have nothing for pain control. Once you thaw out, it is going to hurt; you'll just have to deal with it. Maybe it will make you think twice next time you decide to pull this kind of stunt."

He shot her another look of warning before getting up and going to the kitchen to get a first aid kit and a bowl of warm water. He then went into a box on the mantle and retrieved something she couldn't see and came back to her.

She observed her surroundings for the first time. Looking around, she saw the kitchen with an old double porcelain sink and a small island. There was a dining room table and two chairs, and on the other side of that was another bathroom. The door was open, and she could see there was a shower. The walls were primitive, unfinished, rounded logs, and the window above the sink had white cotton curtains with little yellow daisies. The living room was small, and the stone fireplace took up one whole wall. There was a painting of a classic English fox hunt above it, with the only other decorations or furniture being a braided rug and the chair she sat in. Even under the circumstances, she considered it charming.

He pulled up a footstool from nearby and sat in front of the chair. He washed the cut first, and as the warmth started to return to her foot, it became painful, just like he'd warned her. She sat silent, acting as if it didn't. Trying not to show any weakness, she bit her bottom lip and watched him.

He then produced and opened what looked to be super glue. Pausing for a moment to tell her,

"This is going to hurt. Scream if you want to; there's no one around to hear you."

He pulled the two sides of the cut together with his thumb and forefinger and ran a thick line of glue down it. He held it in place, all the while staring at her.

Allison tilted her head back, stifling a sob. She rested her head on the back of the chair and stared at the ceiling while tears streamed down into her hair. But she remained still and quiet through it all.

After a few minutes of holding it in place, he put duct tape across the cut in layers, the last layer going all of the way around her foot.

When he was done, he got up and grabbed a heavy wool sock and carefully slipped it over her foot and up her calf. He then stoked the fire, added more logs, and went into the kitchen to make tea. She silently watched him. The hate for him growing stronger by the minute.

Allison wasn't sure why she did what she did next.

He brought a tray from the kitchen containing a teapot, two cups, and a sugar bowl and started to place it onto the table beside the chair. Her frustration had come to a boiling point, and she reached over with all of her strength and hit the tray, sending it and all of its contents across the room. Hot tea splattered across his legs, and one teacup hit the fireplace and shattered.

He didn't hesitate. He scooped her up much like one would a sack of potatoes and carried her to the bedroom. He threw her on the bed and wrestled to get her arm still enough to place the wrist cuff on. She wasn't going to make it easy. And when he succeeded in securing one of them, she flailed, making it almost impossible to secure the second.

He straddled her, trying to gain control. After successfully securing her other wrist, he looked down at her, and she spat in his face. The look he shot her made her immediately regret it.

He said through gritted teeth,

"What in the fuck is wrong with you? You really are a piece of work." And then he did something she never saw coming.

Both arms secure above her head, he moved one knee down between her thighs and then the other. Prying her legs apart with his own. Never losing eye contact, he reached down and partially removed his boxers enough to free himself. He growled.

"Is this what you want? It is, ISN'T IT?"

Before she could react, she felt him rock hard. He ripped off her undies and in one swift, experienced move, he licked his hand, briefly grabbed his dick, and burrowed into her. Hard and fast.

She gasped, the pain making it impossible to do anything else. He filled her up, his girth giving her the sensation he would split her in half.

Allison was stunned into silence and immediately aroused.

He sat back on the balls of his feet, not thrusting but instead pulling her onto him. His hands were placed on her hips, micro-controlling each move. Once, twice, and then again. Slowly, until she was completely wet. She glided onto him, and he held her there for a moment. He looked over her, scanning her body, and then fell onto her breasts. Greedily sucking her nipples and biting. He had complete control, and it was painful and exciting. Her restricted arms made it impossible to grab his ass or direct him in any way. She was at his mercy.

He switched tempos—angry and primal. There was no gentleness to his movements. He was fucking her. She looked up to him, his black hair lying in tendrils across his cheeks and down his back, his dark shoulders square and taut, and his muscles tense and defined. His face, which normally remained expressionless, was anything but. His eyes relayed hunger and need. But she didn't have to see it; she *felt* it, and it was the biggest turn-on she had ever experienced.

When she was on the edge of orgasm, he abruptly stopped and pulled out. He grabbed her around her hips and flipped her over. She was face down, with her arms crossed above her head, the silk robe she wore pushed up around her shoulders. Lifting her onto her knees, he positioned himself behind her, and without skipping a beat, he entered her again. That time even harder, forcing her face into the pillow.

He grabbed her hips and squeezed. Allison was backing onto him, pumping with all that she had until she couldn't hold back any more and exploded. Convulsions tightening around him inside of her. He felt her and sped up until he came. Groaning, "*Fuckkkk.*" Before collapsing on her back, forcing them both down onto the bed.

He laid on her, allowing his breathing to become even again before getting up.

Allison didn't move. Her face was still buried in the pillow. After she caught her own breath, she maneuvered herself with her legs and turned over. She studied him as he took a rag and wiped the inside of her thighs and crotch.

"What is your name?" she asked.

He finished what he was doing, threw the blanket over her, and left the room. She assumed he was gone for the night, but he returned a few minutes later. He unlocked one of her wrists and started investigating the ankle strap she had removed.

After realizing he just hadn't had it on her ankle tight enough, he attached it again over the wool sock to the tightest rivet and then released her other arm. She would have trouble walking on that foot anyway. He felt pretty sure there wouldn't be a repeat.

The second time he went to leave, he paused in the doorway and turned to look at her over his shoulder.

"Leo. My name is Leo." He flipped off the light, saying. "Get some sleep."

And then left.

***

Neither of them slept that night. Allison finally gave in to exhaustion just after sunrise. Leo spent those few hours pacing back and forth between the front porch and the cabin. He felt like a caged animal, unsure of what to do. Knowing that he couldn't undo what had been done and beating himself up over it.

She did something to him he didn't understand and couldn't explain. She made him feel out of control and irrational. It was new to him—that inability to contain himself. She made him *feel*, and that was something he had never experienced. Showing emotions was a weakness, and he had mastered control of them long ago. That realization overwhelmed him.

He walked to the bedroom door and stood leaning against the frame, watching her sleep. She really was beautiful. Not just her appearance, but she harbored a fiery fight in her that shone through, making her magnetic. He quietly walked closer to the bed and stood over her.

She was lying on her side, hugging her pillow. Her hair was tangled from not being brushed those last two weeks, and her skin was pale. Her full mouth had the hint of a smile.

He whispered,

"My God, what have I gotten myself into?"

As if she heard him, she moved. Repositioning her free leg and rolling over onto her back. The quilt only partially covered her. His initial reaction was to cover her so that she wouldn't get cold, but he didn't. He found himself looking at the soft mound of hair between her legs. Something she didn't have when she got there.

Before he knew what he was doing, before he overanalyzed or had time to talk himself out of it, he bent over her. He buried his face between her legs and slowly started exploring her with his tongue. There was so much pleasure in her taste.

He felt her awake before she moaned. And then, her hands were in his hair, pulling and pushing as her hips came up to meet him. He alternated between gently sucking and pulling on her lips and licking her hood, prying it back with pressure. Getting more firm each time until she came. The gush of warm fluid on his tongue was too much.

Again, he found himself inside of her, devouring her warmth.

He slowed down and looked at her, pushing her hair from her face. She was flushed from the orgasm—an orgasm he had just given her. He wanted to kiss her, but somehow it just felt too personal, and he refrained. He redirected his eyes to the wall above the bed, trying to focus on anything but how goddamn good it felt. He wanted it to last; he wanted her to cum again. And she did.

She came too quickly, and when he felt her quiver, he couldn't stop himself and immediately followed.

He laid on her for a moment, waiting for the last shutters to calm. Spent and euphoric, he rolled off. Neither of them spoke and laid until their breathing returned to normal. He positioned himself on his side, resting his head in his hand. She stared at the ceiling. Each breath made her chest rise and fall; her skin was splotched with red.

He waited for her to look at him, to say something, or to help him make sense of it. Anything to help him feel less guilty. But that didn't happen.

He sat up, found his boxers, put them on and said,

"I'll go make food."

When he left the room, he heard her run bathwater. And then he heard the sweetest sound.

She was singing. Her voice echoed off of the tiny bathroom walls, carrying it down the hallway and throughout the little house. She was humming a tune he had never heard, and it sounded serene. It sounded happy.

He found himself smiling while he made coffee, eggs, and potatoes.

As he stared out the kitchen window, the season's first snow began to fall, and he knew then with complete certainty that he couldn't kill her.

Nine

The snow fell that day without reserve. From early morning until late afternoon, it came down in thick flurries. When Leo went out to retrieve firewood, he couldn't see further than a few inches in front of his face. By early evening, it was knee-deep on the ground. And still, it continued. It was no ordinary storm. It was a full-blown blizzard, and they were going to be snowed in for an undetermined amount of time.

The cedar tree branches heavy with ice started to take turns falling under the weight, making the otherwise quiet yard around them surprisingly noisy. With each loud crack of a broken limb, Leo jumped. But by dusk, he had become used to it, and the periodic thumps had started to have the opposite effect. It somehow calmed him. A gentle reminder that they were separated from the rest of the world by the thick blanket of snow and virtually zero visibility.

He busied himself in the cabin by sweeping the floor and cleaning up. He showered, shaved, and meticulously trimmed his beard and then went to the deep freezer to select something for supper. He had stocked it with wild game in the months leading up to their arrival and decided to make a simple rabbit stew. He prepared it and placed it on the stove to simmer. He went out to get his guitar from his Jeep and spent some time playing, and when he got bored of that, he wrote in his notebook.

He had started skipping prayer out of guilt. But it is a hard habit to break, especially with nothing else pressing. So, at 3:00 and 5:00, he found himself doing just that. On his knees, worshiping God. A God that, in his mind, had surely turned his back on him.

He did anything and everything he could to keep his mind off of her. But he knew he was just putting off the inevitable. He was going to have to come up with a revised plan, one that did not include injecting her with succinylcholine and depositing her and her car into a body of water.

They were trapped right where they were, and the certainty of that allowed him to slow down and relax. Food wasn't a concern; he had prepared for the worst and had plenty.

Even if he wanted to continue with the original plan, the deadline was another week away. If they expected him to put her into a river or lake and they were frozen over, what was he to do? They would understand the delay. And if they didn't; no one knew where he and Allison were. He made sure of that, even going so far as to ditch his cell phone and remove the OnStar tracker from her car. He hadn't taken any chances.

That, coupled with the unexpected storm, gave him the excuse he needed to put everything on hold. He put it all in the back of his mind, hoping that a solution would come to him before he needed to proceed. He might go stir crazy, but the bottom line was that he had everything he needed to wait it out. And that was enough for the moment—it had to be.

Leo pulled the pocket watch from his jeans and checked the time. It was almost 6 pm. Allison had been asleep since breakfast. He checked on her many times throughout the day, and even when he put an extra blanket on her, she didn't stir. He went over to his backpack, rummaging through it to find a pair of joggers, a sweatshirt, and a hairbrush. Tucking them under his arm, he crept into her room, carefully so as not to make a sound.

He sat on the edge of the bed, briefly watching her before she opened her eyes. The only light was coming from the hallway. They sat silently staring at one another for a few seconds.

"I've brought you something to wear. It has been snowing all day, and I thought you might be cold."

He looked away from her, clearing his throat before continuing.

"If you would like to come to the kitchen to eat some dinner, you can. I mean, I'll let you. If you want, you don't have to. What I mean is, well, I just thought you might want to."

He was stammering and felt foolish. He gave up and stood, unlocked her ankle, and left her to get dressed. Unsure if she would join him or not, he went to the kitchen and stood staring at the pot on the stove.

His stomach was swimming as he tried to collect himself enough to gather bowls and set the table, quickly surveying the kitchen area to make sure there were no knives or anything she could use as a weapon. He wouldn't blame her for taking an opportunity if it was in her face. He didn't put it past her either.

He stashed away the paring knife and turned around just in time to see her hobbling down the hall. She was hopping on her healthy foot and holding onto the wall. His sweatshirt went down to her knees, and it was comical. He couldn't help but smile. It filled him with a ridiculous amount of joy when she smiled back.

Half-hearted as it was, it was still a smile, and he would take it.

She made it as far as the living room chair before she made one final hop and flopped down into it.

"I think there is something wrong with my leg."

It took a minute for what she said to register with him. But when it did, he grabbed the footstool and seated himself in front of her to check it out.

He gently pulled off the sock and knew immediately that she was right. Her leg was swollen and red all of the way to her knee. He got the first aid kit and the scissors, came back, and cut the tape away. Her foot was rather large, and the gash was angry and inflamed. One end of the wound was open and oozed pus. He washed it, dried it, and left it propped up on the stool. Searching through the kit, he found a few oral antibiotics and brought her water to take them.

"You will need more antibiotics, but this should help for now. We need to keep it elevated. I'll bring your food to you."

She looked at him and spoke her first civil words.

"Thank you, Leo."

It almost stopped him in his tracks. Hearing her say his name would take some getting used to.

He brought her a bowl of stew on a tray and set it on her lap. He grabbed his own and took a seat on the hearth a few feet away.

They ate in silence, both trying to get past the awkwardness created by their recent shared experience. It was, by all accounts, a mind-fuck, to be honest.

Somehow, they had gone from captor and captive at war with each other to two people that felt as if they were on a first date. Neither of them had a clue how to act. But one thing was for sure: there was no hate or anger between them at that time. Having sex as complete strangers could have gone either way.

When she finished, he took her bowl to the kitchen, and again she thanked him. While he was cleaning up, Allison was eyeballing his guitar.

"I heard you playing earlier today. You're good."

His back was to her at the sink, and he smiled to himself. He replied,

"Thank you."

He finished up, and after making tea, he returned. They both sat with their cups for a bit before she spoke again. She was staring at the fire and spoke calmly and low. Her hair had been brushed and laid in soft waves down her shoulders. In all of the months he watched her, he couldn't remember ever seeing her wear her hair down. It softened her features and tipped the scales from pretty to gorgeous. She looked and acted like a completely different person.

"What you said. What you said about my husband—is it the truth? Did he hire you to take me? And what did you mean when you said if this doesn't go well, I would be killed anyway?"

Initially, her question stunned him. He hadn't considered having to answer questions about what was happening. He looked down and took his time pondering what his response should be. He didn't want to scare her, and she did deserve to know the truth. But if she somehow managed to escape, he was giving her all of the information she would need to nail him to the cross. He was having an inner dialogue with himself, hashing it all out. Trying to come up with the best possible words. He was conflicted.

She sat in silence, waiting for him to answer, watching him. As if seeing his inner turmoil, she said,

"Please."

He set his cup down and stood up. Resting his arm along the mantle while stoking the fire. He found it difficult to look her in the face and lie, but finally answered,

"Yes, it's the truth."

She looked up at him, seeming to look through him more than at him. Her eyes focused midway down his chest.

"Do you know why?"

Leo could actually answer that question honestly and tried to explain what he could.

"It seems that your husband made some questionable investments. But that isn't the whole story. He gave some bad financial advice to someone pretty high up in the food chain. I am not sure if he knew he was swindling a top boss of the mafia when he took his money, or if his intentions were good and it was just bad luck on some inside trade information. I can only tell you what I know, and what I do know is that if he doesn't pay them back and make this right, he won't live long. He is on borrowed time. That is all of the details I have. I wish I could tell you more."

Allison looked into his eyes. She didn't appear upset; there was no reaction. As if it didn't surprise her. Her voice was flat when she asked,

"How did you get involved? Or is this what you normally do? If you don't mind me asking."

"I'd rather not say. But what I will tell you is

that I didn't do this for financial gain. I am normally a pretty honest guy with no ties to organized crime. I didn't have a choice."

She squinted her eyes and wanted more of an explanation. But he didn't give one, and she looked down at her lap. He could see her mind digesting what he had told her and after a long pause, she said,

"I don't understand. Heath never acted as if he was in trouble. Our bills seem to be paid, and he didn't ever show signs of having a surplus of money either."

She sat for another extended period of time, and Leo saw her face change. As if some hidden knowledge shed some light on the whole situation.

"He has no access to my accounts. He won't be able to pay ransom. Is that why I have been here so long? What happens if he can't pay?"

Her nonchalant demeanor was replaced with what appeared to be panic, making her body rigid and posture upright. Her eyes widened as she told him,

"Even if they kill me, it won't do them any good. I changed the beneficiary of my will and life insurance last year. Heath doesn't stand to get a dime. It all goes to my son Ben."

He understood her new concern and tried to

put her mind at ease.

"You are safe here. I am not going to hurt you, and your son is safe as long as you are still alive."

He saw her shiver and left the room to get a blanket.

But the shiver she experienced wasn't from being cold. It was from something else entirely.

He brought her the blanket, put ointment on her foot, and wrapped it in a soft cloth. He grabbed his guitar from the corner and sat strumming a folk song.

She found a small amount of comfort in what he had told her. For the moment, she was safe. The wind was rattling the windows of the cabin, and the fire crackled, and at some point, she dozed.

Rather than carry her back to the room, Leo brought the quilt and pillows out to the living room, and along with his sleeping bag, he made a pallet on the floor in front of the fire. He laid her down and then stretched out beside her.

As he watched the fire, thinking over the day and their conversation, he couldn't help but feel protective of her. She had done nothing to deserve her current circumstances. She was the casualty of other people's war. He felt a responsibility to fix it. And yet, he had no idea how.

He closed his eyes, tried to calm his mind, and eventually gave into sleep, only to wake a few hours later.

The fire was low, the room cool, and she was snuggled up to his side. He got up and put more logs on, then took his place beside her again. That time he stretched his arm out and pulled her into him. Without waking, she put her head on his chest and her leg over his own. He pulled her tightly into his hug, deeply breathing in the scent of her, and slept. He slept better than he had in years.

Ten

Allison awoke to the morning light coming through the curtains. She saw him lying next to her and quietly got up and limped to the bathroom.

Curiosity led her to look out the window, and she was surprised to see the snow still falling. The powder stopped just short of the bottom kitchen pane. It had to be almost four feet deep. She rummaged around the cabinets looking for coffee to go in the percolator on the stove, but had no luck.

The fire had all but gone out, and the little house was cold. She went back to the pallet and climbed back under the covers.

Propping herself up on her elbow, she looked at him.

He had on a white t-shirt, and his arms laid on top of the covers across his chest. He was built well, with a thick neck and firm muscular body. His skin was dark and smooth, and his curly black hair shone, lying in ringlets on the pillow. She thought back to the day before when she'd seen him smile and recalled the dimples in his cheeks. His lips were full, and at that moment, as he slept, his jaw was slack and his mouth half open. He really was flawless, and she couldn't help herself.

She sat up and reached out to touch him, lightly tracing his bottom lip with her index finger. He didn't move. She did it again, and then timidly leaned in and brushed her lips across his, and he responded. His eyes half open, he grabbed the back of her head, pulling her mouth against his. Softly at first, and then completely.

He sat up and lifted her body until she was straddling him. He kissed her with a warmth and passion she had never before experienced. Making her throbbing leg and foot seem unimportant. If only for a moment.

He felt her wince and pulled away.

"Oh, I'm sorry. Your foot!"

"It's okay. Please don't stop. Please." She pleaded.

It came out as more of a beg than a request, and her hand was already at his waist, pulling and tugging at the button on his jeans.

Leo smiled, holding her against him with one arm while rolling them both over until she was on her back.

She held her arms above her, and he pulled

the sweatshirt over her head. He stared down at her; there was a smolder in her eyes. Some kind of magnetic sparkle that made him delirious.

She had goosebumps from the chill in the air. He stopped, taking a few minutes to stoke what was left of the embers and stack some fresh logs in the grate. Returning to her after he removed his jeans. He pulled her pants off of her, ending up at her feet. He crawled back up, burrowing his way between her legs, pushing them apart until they were as wide as they could go.

He put his arms under her until her ass was cradled in the crook of his elbows and his face was directly above her slit. His tongue slid down between her lips. He stroked her with it slowly. First up and then down. He kept slowly repeating the cycle, the whole time maintaining eye contact.

His arms held her tightly in place, preventing her from moving, and she squirmed. Again, she was under his complete control. What he was doing was borderline annoying, and it was intentional.

When she thought she would lose her mind, he switched and repeated his method from side to side. Still, he didn't speed up or apply more pressure, and he never looked anywhere but directly in her eyes.

Allison tilted her head back and, with equal

amounts of pleasure and frustration, let out a moan.

She saw his eyes dance, as if he were subduing a smile. He was enjoying his little game.

He worked his way down, darting his tongue into her a few times before releasing his hold on her hips and using his fingers. He inserted them and started stroking upwards inside of her, while his mouth worked its magic on the outside. She had never experienced anything quite like that feeling, and it took all of her focus to control herself. She willingly stifled her orgasm.

Leaning forward, she stopped him.

"Wait."

Leo looked confused and asked,

"What's wrong?"

"Nothing, nothing is wrong. But I want..."

He crawled up until their faces were close and kissed her, smearing her face and sharing her flavor from his lips.

"What? What do you want?"

Allison had never been in the position she was in and struggled with verbalizing her desires. She stammered and looked down.

"I want to give you pleasure. I want you; I want to taste you too. I want you in my mouth."

She felt shy and looked at him, searching for a reaction. A slow grin came across his face as he rolled off of her and positioned himself, lying on his back beside her. His arms were locked behind his head.

She hesitated, unsure of how to begin. In all of her years with Heath, it was not something she liked or wanted. The few times she had given him a blow job, he had forced her to do it. Holding her head and ramming it down her throat until she choked and gagged. It was not associated with good memories, and in fact, it felt like a violation. But for some reason, she wanted to do it for Leo. She told him,

"I am not good at it."

He sat up a little, taking her hand and kissing it lightly on the top. Before saying,

"This isn't something someone is good or bad at. Allison, it is an expression of desire. To give someone pleasure is subjective. Each person likes it a different way. We learn it together. You don't have to."

"I want to; I really want to."

He guided her, helped her get into a position between his legs, and when she was on her knees, he told her,

"Do what you like. I assure you that whatever you do will feel good. Take your time and don't be afraid to ask questions."

He leaned back and closed his eyes. Giving her the added comfort of not feeling like she was being observed.

Allison timidly took him into her hand. First kissing the top, lingering there for a moment. Enjoying the feeling of the soft skin on her lips. She ran her tongue down his shaft a few times, getting it wet with her slobber. Gradually she took the head into her mouth, a little at first, and then all of it, swirling her tongue around the edge. She scooted up so that the angle allowed him access further down her throat as she attempted to take him all in. Not wanting to overwhelm her, he laid motionless.

She was not thinking about what he liked as much as she was exploring. The texture, taste, and feeling were new and surprisingly amazing. She was unhurried, which was fine at first but became almost unbearable for him. Slow, methodical torture. He sat up a bit, putting his hands on her shoulders near her neck, applying pressure to let her know when he wished her to go down and then back up. He reached down at the base where her hand was resting, placing his own hand over hers and gently squeezing and guiding it up. It only took her a few minutes to get the idea. She picked up his cues until she had the perfect rhythm and technique. That, coupled with the fact it was new to her, brought him to the edge quickly. Her innocence in that particular area was a complete turn-on.

She was doing to him what he had done to her, and he tried to stop her before the point of no return. But she resisted, pushing his hands away and holding on tighter. She became more aggressive, and so did he. He had to give into his primal urge to thrust harder, grabbing her by the crown of her head and pushing himself to the back of her throat. Still, she didn't come up for air and never gagged. It was more than obvious that she was enjoying herself immensely, and it became too much. He waited too long and didn't have the chance to warn her. He knew instinctively she wouldn't care.

She felt him starting to pulsate in her mouth, a few smaller surges, and then spasms. He let out one last groan as her mouth was filled with warmth. Thick and hot, covering her tongue and shooting down the back of her throat. She didn't stop until he stopped her. His shaking hands held onto her hair, tangled around his fingers. He shivered, pulled himself from her lips, and pushed her back, where he immediately returned the favor.

They laid together in front of the fire, kissing and holding onto one another. Before she climbed up onto him. She was lying with her chest on his stomach and put both hands under her chin and looked up to him. He was stroking her back as she began to ask all of the questions she had held onto those weeks.

Where was he from? How long had he followed her? Did he have a wife or children? Where was his family, and what was his background and education? She had so many questions, and he answered them all to the best of his ability, only keeping to himself the secret that would make her hate him.

He couldn't bring himself to tell her that she was supposed to be killed. He knew he would tell her eventually, but only after he had come up with a solution to the problem. Not a minute sooner.

After she was satisfied with his answers, he asked his own questions. His were more creative. Like, when did she learn to paint, and why had she married Heath? Why didn't she work, and why on Earth had she started taking so much medication or drinking like she did? But mainly he wanted to know why everyone thought she would have the kind of money it would take to make her abduction worth all the trouble.

She explained.

"Well, my parents met very young. They fell in love and got married when they were in their teens. Neither my mother's nor my father's parents would allow it. So, they eloped. They ran away from their home country, immigrating to the United States. They were disowned and disinherited by both sides. Which was fine with them. But it lit a fire under my father. In a way, he spent his life trying to prove to himself that he could create his own fortune and didn't need to depend on anyone else. And he did. He started a company called Dalcon. Have you heard of it?"

Leo couldn't recall that name.

"It is a pharmaceutical company. Anyway, the company did well, and so he started a second company under a different name as competition to the first. Causing the stock in one or the other to always be in his favor. There is more to it than that. He branched out, creating separate businesses that received funding for clinical trials and such, and they too were successful. Our time was spent in between the United States and Sweden, and I always knew they did well. But I didn't realize exactly how well until my mother died almost five years ago."

"My father found out he had terminal cancer and refused treatment, dying from it in less than a year. My mother followed six months later from an unknown illness. Dale and Connie: Theirs was a true love story. My father was her life; without him, she had no will to live. I believe she took something untraceable to put an end to her grief. I was their only child, the sole heir."

Leo considered how his next question would sound but decided to ask anyway.

"How much are you worth?"

Without hesitation, Allison answered,

"On paper, roughly 12.5 million. But I have offshore accounts and property elsewhere that no one knows about. Easily tripling that amount."

He couldn't hide his surprise and audibly gasped.

He hadn't really been worried about what would happen or how it would happen until that minute. That much money would make anyone stupid. He immediately felt panic. He was afraid, not just for her, but for him, if he didn't figure out how to fix the situation.

He tried to act normal, but after a few minutes, she knew something wasn't right. His whole demeanor had changed with the realization that they would never give up. No matter where they went or what they did, if he didn't produce a body, they would be hunted.

"Leo, what is it? You can tell me."

He got up, slipped on his jeans, and went to the kitchen to make coffee. She sat up, pulled the blanket around her chest, and suspiciously watched him.

He put the coffee on and came back, taking a seat in the chair. He was leaning forward with his elbows on his knees when he finally told her. He felt he had no choice.

"I didn't tell you the whole truth."

He peered up at the ceiling before running his hand through his hair. He leaned back to avoid her stare.

"There has been no ransom demand."

She answered,

"What? I don't understand."

"You are supposed to be dead by the end of the week. I guess your husband didn't know you changed your will."

He said it quickly and then let out a long sigh. As bad as it was to say, so much relief came to him by saying it.

Allison turned and blankly stared at the fire.

"Oh, I see."

He had expected anger, but what he got was so much worse. He heard the hurt in her voice. she asked,

"How will I die? How have you planned to kill me, Leo?"

He went to her, sitting beside her and grabbing her thigh.

"Listen, that was then. I won't hurt you, and I would kill anyone who tried. I will figure this out."

"You didn't answer the question. *How were you planning to kill me?*"

Leo leaned back, gazing at the side of her face. Then calmly answered.

"I have a vial of a drug called succinylcholine. It is fast acting and renders…"

She interrupted.

"I know what succinylcholine is."

They both sat quietly for a bit. When she turned and looked at him, his heart almost stopped. Visibly pained, she asked,

"Why would you agree to something like this?"

He answered,

"My father owes the same people that your husband does. I had to agree. To protect my mother and my sister."

"Oh, I understand. So, you have no choice."

Leo grabbed her and folded her into him.

"No. I would never hurt you."

He kissed her on the top of the head.

"So, what happens now?"

"I don't know, but I'll figure it out. It will be okay. Somehow, I will make this okay.

Eleven

The snowstorm seemed to mark the last of Allison's days as a chained-up captive. She was free to roam about the cabin, and they spent those days learning about each other. Trying to bridge the gap that was created by how they'd started out, who they wanted to become, and what was standing in the way.

Even when the snow stopped falling, the sun was slow to melt it away, and so they remained inside, never venturing further than the woodpile stacked outside the door.

Leo prepared most meals and did the chores while she still nursed a swollen leg and foot. Without proper medicine at their disposal, her healing was slow.

In the evenings, they talked, sharing stories of their childhood and core memories. Even though he was a man of few words, he answered whatever she asked and seemed to enjoy listening. They played cards, and he taught her how to play Backgammon. Their familiarity came gradually, but their genuine care for one another seemed to blossom overnight. Even if trust had not.

But no matter what they did to occupy their time, the realization of their inability to come up with a solution always loomed.

It nagged Leo in his sleep and played with his peace. Allison's life was not the only one on the line, and he was running out of time. As the number of days started stacking up behind them, the pressure he was under started manifesting in different ways.

Their sexual encounters became more heated, aggressive, and rough. Bordering on angry or desperate. And each time, they felt closer and more familiar, until they knew each other's desires like they knew their own. Together, they were explosive.

Neither of them was foolish, and both had very real reasons not to trust. And although they gave in to each other sexually, they couldn't imagine a life beyond their current circumstances and held back from anything more. She felt that, in the end, he would have no choice. She had no doubt that he possessed the strength to do what he needed to do.

He was intuitive and knew she didn't trust him. She kept her feelings just outside the danger zone, only opening up and expressing need fueled by passion; nothing more.

Sure, she shared parts of her life, but he could tell she was regretful in telling him how much money was on the line. People do strange things when it comes to needing money or protecting the ones they love. And he had both. And with all that truth tumbling around in her head, she still couldn't stop herself from enjoying him.

His exterior was harsh and cold, but he could be equally tender and gentle. Intelligent, empathetic, and charismatic. She craved his attention and affection. It was confusing, and she had given up on trying to see past it or withholding her needs. She had spent the last twenty years affection-starved. If it was her last week alive, she would enjoy every second. She understood his predicament.

What she didn't realize is that each intimate encounter cultivated true feelings in him. He had gotten to the point that he didn't just want her; he needed her, and the only thing on his mind was how to save them both. The thought of being without her was unacceptable. All of the hours he laid awake when she slept, every moment he spent in the kitchen or strumming his guitar, was time spent trying to formulate a plausible plan. It had become his only concern. Not only to save everyone involved, but to have her as his own.

It made those days pass too quickly, and his panic became obvious.

It was Wednesday evening when he unexpectedly got out of the shower one evening and began to dress. Putting on his thick winter socks and flannel shirt and collecting things to put in his rucksack. Allison silently watched him, waiting for an explanation. Before he grabbed his coat, he sat down at the kitchen table and told her,

"Listen, I have to go to the city tonight. I have to touch base with these people, or they will assume I've failed, and I can only imagine what will happen. I can't risk it. I will be gone until tomorrow."

She sat for a moment and then nodded her understanding. He continued.

"Allison, I am going to need to secure you again. Please understand. I am not doing it for punishment or to be cruel, but I think you can understand that I don't feel like I have a choice. It is for your own protection."

She didn't immediately respond. It took her a few minutes to digest the fact she would be going back to the room where she was held captive to be put in chains again. She blankly stared at him for a moment before standing.

As she started towards the bedroom, he

grabbed her arm. He held her there, looking into her eyes.

"I'm going to need you to trust me."

She stared at him.

Looking down, she nodded her head yes, and he followed her to the room. After looking at her swollen calf and oozing foot, he placed the leg cuff around her healthy ankle.

"I will bring back medicine and dressing."

Before he left, he opened the curtain and placed some things on the bedside table. A cup, a thermos of tea, crackers, some trail mix, and what looked to be a few sandwiches. He left and came back with the deck of cards and a small notebook and pencil. Lastly, he placed a stack of blankets on the foot of the bed.

She rolled over and faced the window. He stood over her and said,

"I'll be back soon."

And then he left. Leaving her alone with her thoughts for the first time in almost a month. When the sound of his Jeep faded away, she hugged her pillow and cried.

***

The ice had cleared, and once he got off of the back roads and onto the highway, it was normal traveling. Leo made it into Washington just after sunrise on Thursday. First going to the bus station in Olympia. There inside of a locker he had stashed a cell phone and cash. He pocketed the money and made the call, explaining that the storm had put him behind in the overall schedule but promising they would have a body by the following weekend. They accepted the update that bought him more time, and it brought him a small amount of relief.

After finding a place to get bandages and antibiotics for Allison, he stopped into a cafe to grab a bite. He sat eating his eggs and toast in a fatigued stupor until he heard something that snapped him out of it.

He heard Allison's name and looked up at the old television on the coffee bar, where he saw a picture of her across the screen. He set down his fork and struggled to swallow his mouthful of food.

The waitress was standing a few feet away with the remote in her hand. Even though the sound and captions were on, she turned it up. He saw that the news reporter was filming in front of Allison's house, and Heath was standing just behind her. Leo felt sick to his stomach as he watched her husband step forward with tears in his eyes and plead for the public's help in finding his "beloved wife."

He was so caught up in watching it, he let out a short "*Hhm*!" followed by "asshole" under his breath. But he must have been louder than he thought, because the waitress turned around and looked at him.

She was around thirty and wore a t-shirt with the *'Barney's Bacon and Breakfast'* logo on it. Her hair was in a ponytail, and she had entirely too much makeup on for that time of day. She looked him over before speaking.

"Yeah, bet that woman is dead, and I bet anything her husband did it."

Leo awkwardly stared at her.

Guilt is a strange thing. It has a tendency to make a person want to be invisible but feel more seen than ever before. He wondered how she had come to that conclusion. More than that, he marveled at the fact she was spot on in her suspicion of Heath. He couldn't think of anything to say but finally managed,

"Yeah, probably so."

As he stood to go, he finished his cup of coffee and couldn't get out of there fast enough.

He had come up with a plan and needed to get to the other side of the city.

It was a simple plan, really. He would find someone on the edge of society, someone who wouldn't be missed. A female's body that could be burned and could pass as Allison.

He drove to the area just outside of the city. It was a popular place for prostitutes, peddlers, and addicts.

Pulling onto a street with neglected houses and unkempt yards, he was immediately approached. There were groups of women gathered on the corner around a street lamp, and one of them came up to his slow-moving Jeep.

Although he had hatched a plan, it was not a well-thought-out one, and as the middle-aged, fatigued-looking woman opened the door and tried to get in, he realized that it wouldn't be that easy. He would need to go through a process of hanging back somewhere and observing people until he found a subject that would work. Daylight in the area wasn't ideal, and he hadn't even brought the syringe.

He waved her away and sped off, trying to regroup and fine-tune his original idea. As he headed out of town, he decided on a different approach. It would be better to find a woman in Oregon and cross back into Washington to dispose of her. That way, if she was missed, being in a different state would make it harder for law enforcement to connect the dots. He needed to get back to the cabin and would work it all out there. He had another seven to ten days to make it happen and was concerned for Allison.

He got onto the interstate, lost in his own thoughts. As he merged with the traffic, he glanced into his rearview mirror and noticed a police car behind him. He experienced an immediate rush of panic as he saw the red and blue lights go on.

He was being pulled over.

"What the hell?" he said out loud as he pulled onto the shoulder of the highway.

By the time the officer approached his window, he already had his insurance and registration in his hand. The policeman asked him for his license and when he reached to his glove box to get it, he said,

"Careful to keep your hands where I can see them."

It didn't surprise him. He had dealt with law enforcement on several occasions, and they always had the same reaction. He knew his size and appearance were somewhat intimidating. It is just how it was. He slowed his movements. He didn't need any trouble and would do whatever he needed to so that he could get back on the road. He wanted to ask why he had been pulled over, but from experience he knew better.

After handing him his paperwork, the cop said,

"I've pulled you over today because you just left an area known for drugs. Also, you didn't signal when you merged and seemed to swerve. Have you had anything to drink today?"

Thinking to himself, the fewer words, the better, Leo answered,

"No."

"Alright, hang tight. I'll be back."

Leo watched him in his rearview mirror. After a longer wait than anticipated, he observed another police car arrive and his nerves kicked in.

He saw the first officer get out of his car and have a conversation with the second. And then they both came back to him. One on the driver's side and one on the passenger side. When the original one reached his window, he asked him to step out of the vehicle. Leo was confused but complied.

The first officer asked,

"Do you have anything illegal in the vehicle?"

Leo answered,

"Of course not."

"Do you give your consent for me to take a look?"

"Do what you need to."

He stood on the side of the highway with the

second officer while the first one searched. After a few minutes of rummaging, they were convinced he was clean. But that fact wasn't going to change anything. And when he was finished, he came to Leo, handed back his paperwork and said,

"Mr. Weiss, you have quite a few outstanding traffic tickets. And I would be happy to let you go with a promise to return and pay the court, but I can't. You have a warrant out for your arrest in Lincoln County. I have to take you in."

Leo stood shocked.

"You're taking me to jail?"

"Yes, sir. Turn around and place your hands behind your back."

Not wanting to make things worse, he did what he was told but asked.

"When can I pay the ticket? How long will this take?"

As he placed the handcuffs on his wrists, he told him,

"Normally you could do it the same day with an eight-hour turnaround, but that isn't the case today. By the time you get booked, it will be this evening. It's a holiday weekend. The courts are closed, and the judge won't be back until Monday."

Oh my God, he thought to himself—*Allison.*

Twelve

That first night alone was the most restless Allison had spent since being brought there. She tossed and turned, never really sleeping. By the next morning, it was absolutely freezing inside. She was under all of the blankets and covers, trying to stay warm. The view from her window was gray and dismal.

She opened the thermos of tea that had become lukewarm and drank it with a handful of trail mix and a few crackers. She had no idea what time it was or when he would be back. She held out hope it would be before nightfall.

Seeing her leg that morning brought her pure anxiety. Her ankle was the size of her calf and swollen all of the way to her thigh. She hobbled to the toilet on her healthy one, dragging the chain behind her. It was more difficult than having it on the foot that was injured.

In hopes of washing it, she turned on the bathtub faucet. It sputtered and delivered a small amount of rusty brown water before making a whining noise and then stopping altogether. She tried the tap on the sink.

Nothing. No clean water. Frustrated, she resigned herself to the fact she would have to wait for Leo and limped back to bed.

With nothing to do, she did what she couldn't do at night and slept. Rolling over a few times during the day to unwrap the foil and eat one of what turned out to be bologna and cheese sandwiches. When she awoke again, it was dark, with only the light of the moon coming through her window. She ate the other sandwich, drank the rest of the tea, and when she woke again, it was another day, and Leo still wasn't back.

By mid-afternoon, she was riddled with fear and concern. He had led her to believe he wouldn't be that long. He should have already been back.

That is when she realized she honestly had no idea how far he was going or even where she was. She started reviewing the last few weeks, going through her mind for clues as to where the cabin was. No answers.

She remembered the night she tried to escape. The trees were tall and skinny, appearing to be ash and cedar. Both were an uncommon part of the landscape in Washington. She also didn't notice many pine or oak trees. Taking into account that it was dark, she still had to consider that maybe she was in a different state entirely.

Her mind started replaying everything as her world became filled with more and more doubt.

Maybe he hadn't come back on purpose?

She quickly dismissed that idea, knowing that if he had told her the truth, his family would be in danger if he didn't. She considered every explanation, including the scenario where he had been captured and killed by the Mafia. And what if they decided to come finish the job themselves? She tried to put such things out of her mind, but she knew something was wrong. It had been two days, and she had no access to water, and she was down to a few crackers and a handful of trail mix. But worse than that, she felt feverish. The infection from her foot was making her sick, and she had no way to even wash it.

She uncovered her legs, looking first at the wound and then at the one wearing the ankle cuff. It was leather, and he had fastened it to the tightest rung. The strap went over a u-shaped iron clasp with a padlock. Even though she had done it before, she most certainly couldn't try without water. Escape was impossible. She had no choice but to wait it out.

She laid back on the bed and stared at the ceiling. The magnitude of the situation was overwhelming, and she eventually cried herself to sleep.

By the third day, her fever had escalated, and the pain from the swelling was almost unbearable. She put a pillow under her ankle and ate the remainder of the crackers and trail mix but needed water.

Midday, she watched from her bed as it began to snow again. Icicles formed and hung from the window frame, giving her an idea. If she could get them down, she could suck on them or wait for them to melt in her cup.

Weak and feverish, she got out of bed. After scooting the nightstand under the window to stand on, she saw that there was no way to open it. It looked to be nailed shut. Hoping to break it, she hit it with her thermos. It didn't budge. She aimed higher up, where the glass was weaker without the support of the frame, but still couldn't break it. She reared back and hit it one final time, concentrating all of her weight and using both arms. She heard it shatter and then felt excruciating pain. As if a lightning bolt traveled up her arm and through her shoulder.

She toppled down off of the nightstand, landing on her side, eye level with her left arm. There was a shard of glass protruding diagonally from her forearm, and blood had already started trickling down onto the floorboard. She knew she was in trouble. She laid for a moment, not wanting to accept what was clearly in front of her.

She gradually sat up, leaving the embedded glass where it was, and limped to the bathroom. Sitting on the toilet, she grabbed a towel before gaining enough courage to yank it out. The sound of her own scream was startling as it echoed in the tiny space.

She wrapped her arm and applied pressure, and when the towel was soaked with her own blood, she grabbed her robe. She removed the tie from around the waist and tightly secured it just above her elbow. After a few minutes, the bleeding seemed to stop, but the cut ran deep.

Not having the energy to figure out what to do next, she went back to the bed and crawled under the covers. She was freezing and exhausted. Not just physically, but mentally and emotionally. As the room filled with outside air, she covered her head with the heavy blanket and slept.

***

It would be three more days before Leo was finally free. He had been incarcerated at the county jail until Monday morning before seeing a judge. His bail was set, but he had to be transported to the county that held the warrant. By Tuesday morning, he was beside himself with worry and could think of nothing but getting back to Allison. He paid the fine with the money he had from his locker and took a bus to Central Station to get his Jeep out of impound. If nothing else stood in his way, he would reach the cabin by midnight. He had been gone just shy of a week, and he was desperate to get back.

He had almost lost his mind being locked up. With nothing but time on his hands, all he could think about was her. Did she freeze to death, or had she found a way out of the leg iron and gotten free?

Both scenarios brought him grief and an unbelievable amount of fear. He felt that if she had gotten free, she would have had plenty of time to find her way off of the mountain. But if that were the case, surely she would have alerted someone to what had happened to her, and he would still be in jail facing much more dire consequences. That thought alone gave him enough strength to keep driving in the direction of the cabin.

As he began the ascent, the heavy snowfall slowed his pace and reminded him of why he had purchased a Jeep to begin with. Anything less than a four-wheel drive wouldn't have made it.

He pulled up in front of the cabin at 1:00 am. Unsure of what he would find, he didn't rush in like he had imagined those last few days but walked timidly and unsure. Taking in everything that he saw along the way as clues to what he might find.

The house was colder inside than it was out, but before he built a fire, he went into the bedroom. It was dark, and he felt a breeze. Turning the light on, he saw the window shattered and dark stains on the floor. Her body was under the covers, and he was scared to peel them back.

When he did, she didn't move. He placed his hand on her shoulder and shook her, and she opened her eyes. Her lips were gray and her cheeks flushed. He reached up to touch her skin and felt the heat. She was burning up.

Leo was confused to see a tie on her bicep, but after scanning the room again and taking in the clues, he quickly put it together.

She laid listless as he reached down to turn her arm over. He sat staring at the wound for a moment. It was crusted over with old blood and the beginnings of a scab, but even that didn't disguise the severity of the puncture. Her arm was large, and the skin was tight and yellow around the cut. He told her,

"I'm sorry. I'm so sorry."

He got up and went to the bathroom sink to get her water and saw that it wasn't working. The realization hit him that she had gone without water, but for how long?

"Allison, how long have you been without water?"

She stared at him as if he were an apparition, not answering at first. Then in a whisper,

"The whole time."

His mind began to race as he understood that the broken window wasn't an effort to escape but an attempt for water. He was ashamed.

He covered her and went outside to the well pump and saw that it was frozen over. It took him a while to chip away at the ice enough to free the mechanism so that it would start. After giving her a drink, he built a fire and put some soup on the stove to warm as well as the kettle for tea.

He removed the ankle strap, collected her along with the blankets, and moved her to the living room. He left her to warm up while he nailed a quilt over the window. A temporary fix until daylight.

He spoon-fed her soup and tea before giving her the ibuprofen and antibiotics he'd picked up in the city and then began to tend to her wounds.

Her foot was infected. After submerging it in a warm bath of Epsom salt, he turned his attention to her arm. It was a puncture, not as wide as it was deep. It had crusted over but still oozed. After irrigating it with warm water and hydrogen peroxide, he did the only thing he could. He repeated the steps he had taken originally on her foot and glued the skin together. Other than being swollen and bruised, it didn't appear to be infected. The cold temperature in the bedroom probably had some factor in that. Warmth is a breeding ground for infection. He wrapped it in a layer of gauze.

Drying off her foot, he saw that it looked much worse than it had when he left. He put a thick line of ointment on it and a thin wrapping of bandage. Her body would have to fight it from the inside out. Oral antibiotics would be the only way.

When he'd done all that he could do, he made a pallet on the floor and laid her down. She had been in and out of consciousness during all of it but hadn't asked him any questions. She was dehydrated, feverish, and wracked with infection. She needed a doctor.

He lit a cigarette and sat in the chair watching her sleep. His chest felt tight, and his lungs seemed to struggle to take in air. There had been a lump in his throat for a week, and the relief he should have felt being back was nowhere to be found. Instead, he felt guilt and confusion. How had he let this happen? Not just leaving another human being in that position, but all of it. The whole situation.

By telling his father he would take care of it, he had made a promise he couldn't keep. He had sacrificed his morals and integrity to do something he knew would surely send him straight to hell, and he had somehow justified it in his mind to make it okay. He had signed up for failure. Either he would die, Allison would die, or his family would. And somehow, just a few weeks earlier, her dying had been okay with him. And at his own hands!

Anger propelled him out of the chair and to the porch. His mind was racing, and his frustration and self-loathing consumed him. He found himself in unfamiliar territory. And when he couldn't make sense of his thoughts or feelings, he slowly began to understand why. As if a light bulb went on and it was illuminated. In his face—with no way to ignore the truth.

Maybe this is what love felt like? Did he love her? Was the thought so ridiculous? To him, it was. But all of a sudden, he knew it to be fact.

He shook his head at his own ignorance, and as he became convinced, he needed to hear himself say it. He said out loud,

"I love her."

Hearing the words brought a smile. But as he said them again, he became quite uncomfortable and fearful. Not just of his feelings, but for the very real chance of losing her.

STOCKHOLM SYNDROME: Noun. Feelings of trust and affection felt in many cases of kidnapping or hostage-taking by a victim towards a captor; named with reference to a bank robbery in 1970s Stockholm.

~Oxford Languages

Thirteen

Five days. Leo had five days to figure it out.

While trying to nurse Allison back to health, he planned. From morning till night, he put things in order in his mind. He needed to have everything perfectly thought out, including anything that could go wrong. He looked at the situation from every angle and considered every reasonable way out. And still, there was only one.

By Saturday, she was getting better. Her arm, although sore and still a bit swollen, had formed a thick scab that joined the flesh together. Some of the swelling had subsided in her foot; it was no longer weeping, and her fever was down. Although she was still weak, the antibiotics were doing their job, and he felt relieved. She was lucky to be alive.

His guilt over leaving her in that situation stayed with him through the week, and he couldn't do enough for her. He explained what had happened, and she understood, but it still made him hyper-focused on making her comfortable and healthy. Even though those days were tainted with worry, they were still some of the happiest for them both.

Once he realized how he felt, he came to terms with it and gave in. He had never done that before. No other woman in his life had invoked the caring, gentle side of him, and it felt strange. As if he was learning who he was for the first time.

It wasn't just he who had changed. As Allison felt better, she too found herself reacting to him in a way that was unlike her. She felt safe and valued, wanting to be kind to him. As she watched him tend to her, it wasn't just gratitude she was experiencing. It was something much deeper—something new and different. Something that set her heart and mind at ease. At some point she realized that she did trust him, and that was something she couldn't say about anyone else in the world other than her son Ben.

Leo didn't just take care of her physically, but each thing he did was done with a tenderness that spoke volumes, and she began to open her heart to him.

He ran baths and washed her hair. Served her meals and carried her from one place to the other. He softly kissed her forehead and stroked her hand or arm while they spoke. She felt what he wasn't saying; he didn't need to tell her. And although their circumstances were far from normal or ideal, they both threw themselves into one another. As if they were experiencing their last days together.

And then the time came when Leo had to take action. It was Saturday night, and he couldn't put it off any longer. They had dinner together, and after he had read to her for a while, he closed the book and told her.

"I have to leave again. I think you know why."

He stared at her for a moment, catching her eyes before she turned to look at the fire. She bit her bottom lip but didn't speak.

"I will not tether you to the bed, or anywhere for that matter. Ever again. You will be free to do what you want while I am gone. I will just have to trust that you understand you will have your life in your own hands."

She still didn't speak but leaned forward, grabbing his hand in hers. Silently showing her relief in his decision.

"I have prepared meals and left them in the refrigerator for you. You will have to heat them up. If you need more, look in the freezer; there's plenty. I have also stored water in containers in case the well pump decides to give out again. Your medicine is on the counter; please don't forget to take it three times a day. Tell me you will."

She looked away so that he didn't see the concern and fear in her eyes. A tear slid down her cheek.

"Allison, tell me you will take your medicine. It is important."

"I will. I promise. How long will you be gone?"

Leo sighed, puffing out his cheeks as he exhaled. He squeezed her hand and answered.

"Today is Saturday; I hope to be back by Tuesday."

She wanted to ask questions but intuitively knew he wouldn't answer. He was in full protection mode when it came to her, and even though he hadn't shared anything, she had an idea concerning his plans. Simply because she couldn't think of any other way.

She imagined he would use another body, and honestly, she didn't want to know. To think he could hurt anyone, even if it was to save her life, was too much for her to comprehend. So, she didn't ask.

He let go of her hand and got up. She watched him as he collected things and put them in a bag. He went outside, and she heard him doing something with the Jeep but was unclear what it might be.

A few minutes later he returned, putting things from her console in the Audi down on the table beside the chair. He brought in her duffel bag that she always kept in the trunk for the gym. Lastly, he placed a thick tree limb beside her. Three feet in length, and it appeared to be polished.

"Use this when you walk; try to keep your weight off of that foot."

Squatting down and taking her hand in his, he said,

"Listen, if I am not back by Wednesday, it means I won't be back. We are miles away from anyone. It would take all day to go down the mountain on foot, but if you find yourself needing to, follow it all of the way and take a left at the bottom. Eventually you will come up to a paved road. But do not do anything until Wednesday; give me until then."

He kissed the back of her hand and got up to leave. Stopping a few feet away, like he had forgotten to tell her something.

But he didn't speak again and quickly left the cabin.

As she heard him start the Jeep to leave, she got up and, with the aid of her new makeshift cane, made it to the front door. As he pulled away, she saw that he had her Audi attached to a tow bar on his Jeep.

Of course, she thought. He had to dispose of it as well.

As she watched her blue car fade from sight, she felt a sick feeling in the pit of her stomach. And then she did something she had never done before. She spoke to God.

"Please protect him and bring him back."

***

Right inside the Oregon-Washington border, there was a junkyard. A few acres, occupying a corner lot with rows upon rows of vehicles, out-of-date industrial appliances, and scrap metal. It had long since been abandoned, and the yellow grass grew tall, blurring much of it from view. Flanked by a thickly wooded area, it could only be reached by a dirt road.

As a teen, Leo and his brother used to go there to sell scrap metal or things they had illegally obtained for extra cash. His brother always seemed to have ways in those days to support his addiction, little tricks he had picked up along the way.

When his habit became more of a need than a want, his scruples became nil, and Leo was too young to understand then that anything he did during that time was merely to prevent sickness. He had been unaware that what they were doing was illegal and was usually just along for the ride.

The memory made Leo cringe. But as much as he judged his sibling, the truth was that he had never known him to intentionally hurt anyone like he was about to; his harm had been focused solely on himself. The thought of being worse than him made him sick to his stomach—but not enough for him to reconsider.

He backed in and dropped the Audi. Strategically placing it between a tractor trailer and rusted farm equipment, then covering it with an old tarp. He knew it would be fine there temporarily.

Driving on, he found a motel just before sunrise. He needed a place to rest and regroup, and he couldn't really do anything before nightfall. There was a certain amount of safety that came with darkness. As well as the fact that the type of woman he was in search of wouldn't be available until then.

After paying for a room and getting the key,

he parked his Jeep toward the short end of the long "L"-shaped building. The motel shared the parking lot with a small diner positioned near the main entrance.

As he grabbed his bag and walked to number #12, he glanced over at room #14 and noticed someone standing just inside the open door. There was a female figure in the shadows smoking a cigarette.

A brown puppy bounded out the door towards him, dragging a leash. Just as the scruffy little ball of fur made it to the door between them, she stepped on the cord, jolting him to an abrupt halt. Leo tilted his chin up in acknowledgment and entered his room in a cloud of the unknown woman's cheap perfume.

He threw his things on the bed, washed his face and hands, and flipped on the television. Allison was still making headlines. After a few minutes of failing to find anything other than news, he turned it back off, choosing peace over anxiety. He didn't need anything else wracking his nerves; he was doing that just fine on his own.

He was surrounded by 1980's decor, to include lacquer furnishings marred with burn marks and teal drapes that had probably never been washed. Cockroaches infested the small area, and it smelled like mold. Relaxing enough to sleep was going to be a feat in itself.

He rolled a cigarette and stepped outside briefly to smoke it. There was no sign of the woman from earlier, and he stood smoking with a heightened sense of awareness. He felt as if he was being watched. He surveyed his surroundings and saw no one but couldn't shake the feeling.

Blaming it on his recent propensity for paranoia, he shrugged it off and went inside again, locking the door behind him.

The sun was coming up, but the curtains were heavy and did a good job blocking out the world. Leo laid for a while in the dim room, staring at the ceiling.

He thought about his family and what would happen if he didn't do what he had promised. And then he considered how they would feel about him if they knew what he was about to do. Would he somehow be viewed as an abomination or a horrible person instead of a loving son who saw no other way? If he were caught, would they turn their backs on him, consider him lost, and forget he had ever existed?

He thought about his brother and how much of a disappointment he'd been to his parents. How they struggled with his behavior while he was alive and then the heartbreak and loss after his death. He thought about how their lives would change if he did somehow get captured, charged, and incarcerated. The shock of it, the embarrassment, and the hurt. In their eyes, he had always been the good son. His mind was a carousel spinning around. He thought of it all again and again.

But mostly, he thought about Allison.

Not that her life was more important to him than theirs, but they were his past and she was his future. He knew that with complete certainty but still struggled against it, not knowing what kind of future with her was possible. And even if his family was safe from harm, he knew he would do it anyway.

At some point her soul had attained equal value. She was worth the risk and worth saving. She was worth everything—even Hell. That was something undebatable.

He wasn't sure how, but she had awakened something in him once dormant. He only knew he couldn't go back to the way he was before. He was glad of it, and nothing seemed impossible. He dozed off, more convinced than ever before about anything.

When he woke hours later, he immediately began getting ready for the night ahead of him. What he viewed as the final steps to freedom for all of them.

He sifted through his bag and found the bottle of medicine. After filling the syringe, he put it in the toiletry case and back in his pack, then placed the bottle in his jacket pocket for easy disposal. He needed to destroy it on the side of a highway somewhere, or maybe at the junkyard when he picked up the Audi.

He took a shower, dressed, and then walked across the parking lot to the diner for a bite. Needing coffee more than food, he lingered a bit at his table after eating and drank a second cup. Taking notice that he wasn't as nervous as he should be. It was a job that needed to be done, and knowing it was about to be behind him calmed him.

The only concern being that he would be able to accomplish all that needed to be done within forty-eight hours. But he didn't let the doubt creep in and remained sure of his success. He paid for his food and walked across the cold parking lot back to his room.

When he reached his door, he knew something wasn't right. Pausing there with his key in his hand, he looked to closed door #14. There was no sign of her, but he could smell her. Putting his key in the lock, he turned it slowly.

He opened the door and stood just inside. Something felt off, and the air was thick with perfume. Initially nothing looked out of place, but he knew someone had been in his room. He quickly looked around, walking into the bathroom and taking everything into account.

The proof he needed was in his bag, still exactly where he'd left it, but upon closer inspection, in complete disarray. The one thing that was missing sent him into a panic. The toiletry case was gone, and it wasn't the missing extra cash that had him concerned. He stepped back outside, looking one way and then the other. When he was convinced it was safe, he went to door #14.

He knocked and, after getting no response, turned the knob. It was locked. He retrieved a credit card from his wallet and jimmied it between the frame and the catch. It only took a few passes before it opened. He swung the door in a little, and when there was no sign of protest, he slid in as quickly as he could, closing it behind him.

On the floor in front of the bed was a woman. She was slumped over, her arm tied off with an elastic strip, the syringe he'd loaded earlier still partially hanging from the crook of her arm, her hands balled up in involuntary constriction. The puppy from earlier was a few feet away, tied to the leg of a chair, hopping and whining, struggling to get free.

After the initial shock wore off, Leo locked

the door and moved closer. 70 of the 90 units were gone, her lips were blue, and her vacant brown eyes stared at the ceiling.

Grabbing her lifeless wrist, he felt no pulse.

He sat back on his heels, still taking it all in.

She looked to be in her mid, if not late, forties. Fair skin leather in texture hung from her frame. Track marks ran down each vein of her forearms and biceps, creating intricate purple patterns resembling lightning bolts. As cold as it was outside, she was wearing only a tank top and jeans. Her head was unnaturally cocked to the side, foamy froth leaked from the corner of her mouth, her upper denture hung loosely, protruding past her top lip, and a thick line of black mascara ran down her right cheek.

Around the room and in open view, drug paraphernalia was scattered about. Spoons, lighters, crack pipes, old syringes, and empty baggies. Day-old takeout sat on her cluttered nightstand, and the floor was dotted with trash. The space smelled strongly of vomit and urine, and—there in front of him sat a dead woman he had never met.

The fact that an addict would assume a loaded syringe was fair game boggled his mind. The desperation of such an act was incomprehensible.

He made sense of it the only way he could. Surely it couldn't be simple luck.

It was as if God had somehow intercepted and helped things along. As preposterous as it should have seemed, he saw it as a sign, and any guilt or apprehension he had battled before melted away into relief.

He had a body, delivered to him on a silver platter. He would burn her in the car, making identification difficult, if even possible at all. He carried with him a towel soaked with Allison's blood. He would leave it near the scene.

It was a good plan. He started doing what he needed to do to execute it. He did it calmly and with a sick sense of gratitude. The odds appeared to be in his favor.

Fourteen

Leo quietly slipped into the cabin. Allison was asleep in the chair, her leg resting on the footstool.

It was mid-afternoon, and he had been gone a little less than 72 hours.

His heavy footsteps startled her awake.

She wore a look of disbelief as he walked toward her and opened his coat to reveal the brown ball of fur who was trying desperately to get down.

A slow smile spread across her face, and she reached out for the puppy.

Leo handed him over and knelt down beside the chair, watching her coo over the little guy. He reached out and scratched him behind his ears.

"Oh, my goodness! He's adorable!"

The dog cowered a bit at all of the attention, then burrowed his head into her armpit.

They both laughed.

"I'm not even going to ask," she said.

He stood, and looking down at the pair, said,

"I know he's not a replacement."

Then paused and looked away.

"I want you to know that I didn't hurt her."

He didn't need to elaborate; she knew exactly what he was saying. Her mind went through a set of scenes she had tried to avoid revisiting. Memories of her beloved Trixie; she fought back tears. She'd already suspected Heath had done it. She shook her head to rid herself of the anguish and anger.

And then she felt odd.

Her intuition told her it was over and that Leo had accomplished what he had set out to do.

She didn't want to know the details but still wasn't quite sure how to act.

Was she now sharing space with a murderer? And if so, did she have the right to judge or hold it against him?

After all, had he done the deed, it would be the only reason she would remain alive. What a strange dilemma.

She watched as he removed his boots and hung up his coat, looking for any telltale signs to be positive, one way or another.

The puppy was getting anxious and spun half circles a few times before jumping down. He sniffed his way along the floor, the hearth, the rug, and then to the kitchen, focusing on the area under the table.

Leo reached into the refrigerator and pulled out some leftover stew, placing the whole pan in front of him. He ate it greedily.

They both watched him for a bit before he asked her,

"What should we call him?"

Allison's mind was everywhere *except* on what to name the dog. It took her a while to absorb his words and much longer to answer.

He stood staring at her, waiting.

He could see the turmoil.

He knew what she must think, but no matter what was going on in her head, he shouldn't correct her. He needed her to stay dumb. To all of it. It was the most protective thing he could do.

Exactly what he was protecting her from at that point wasn't clear. He had done everything in his power to leave no traces and no evidence, and he felt confident that no matter what, there was no way anyone could ever tie him to the crime.

He had waited until after dark to load the dead woman's small frame into her own suitcase. He cleaned up and made it look as if she had vacated on her own, placing the remnants of narcotics baggies and other paraphernalia into a trash can in her room. He wanted the hotel maid to be aware of her addiction.

Addicts disappear all of the time.

He'd decided to carry her into Washington after all. He needed her to be discovered. He was counting on it. For all of them.

On the edge of a cliffside, overlooking an old landfill, he had burned the Audi with the unknown woman in the trunk.

It took a lot longer than expected, and he returned later to make sure the fire had done its job. All that was left was a smoldering frame and charred remains. he made the call, and with the single sentence,

"It is done."

He was free to head back to Oregon.

He figured it would take a couple of days to be discovered by authorities, and all would be well.

Leo put the kettle on for tea and nervously wiped imaginary crumbs from the counter. He hadn't really had time to feel regret or guilt until she was there in front of him. Silently accusing.

He stopped long enough to pour the tea, lingering as he stirred in the sugar, still battling with himself about whether to tell her anything.

He needed her to know that she was safe. He wanted desperately to reveal that he hadn't killed anyone and that he wasn't the horrible man she must surely think him to be. Her opinion of him was important, but her plausible deniability was more so.

The puppy had finished the stew and was licking the pan as it scooted across the floor.

"Alright, alright."

He patted the dog on the head and took the pan, placing it in the sink to be washed.

He handed Allison her cup and stoked the fireplace before taking a seat on the hearth. His shoulders heavy, he slumped forward, resting his chest against his knees. As if trying to release some of the weight he had carried those last few days. He buried his head in his hands, rubbed his eyes, and let out a groan before speaking.

He hadn't intended to say much, but before he knew it, words were spilling out of him.

As he began, Allison spoke up.

"Wait."

Looking down at her lap, she said,

"I don't want to know. Please don't tell me."

Ignoring her request, he began again.

"Allison, I didn't kill anyone. I would have, but I didn't have to."

Her look of confusion was more animated than ever, she said.

"I don't understand."

He told her the story with as little detail and as quickly as possible so that he could get to what he felt like was the most important part.

It wasn't about the ease in which everything played out, the luck in how similar the woman looked to Allison, or the fact she had killed *herself.* It wasn't about how all the evidence went up in flames with her Audi or how he'd had the added assurance of destroying the woman's dentures, leaving no way for a dental examination to be performed. It wasn't even about the fact he was able to return ten hours later to make sure there was nothing tangible left without being spotted.

None of that mattered anymore. It was done—behind them.

It was more about the part he knew she needed to hear. The part where he'd gone to Ben's house.

Yes, he had gone to her son's house to warn

him.

He was able to sneak in and out in less than ten minutes, leaving a note that simply said,

"YOU'RE IN DANGER."

It was the best he could do under the circumstances.

He knew the gravity of leaving it inside of his house would be felt enough to get the point across. A well-thought-out added touch to make him aware and cautious.

When he finished telling her everything he thought to be relevant, he sighed and finished his tea. His whole body appeared to relax. She could see the release of the pent-up tension.

She wasn't sure if it was because it was all over or because he was able to verbalize it to someone, but whichever it was, his relief was obvious.

He looked at her for what seemed an eternity to him.

He needed her to respond. To say anything. Good or bad, it didn't matter; he just needed to hear her.

She said nothing but moved from the chair and walked to the hearth, seating herself in front of him and placing her head on his lap.

She began crying. She held onto the outside

of his knees and sobbed.

It was a cry of relief, of understanding, and of safety. All relayed through the release of her tears.

He stroked her hair and let her.

It felt foreign to him—consoling someone.

He found himself wanting to cry with her. But he held firm and just sat silently, running his hands through her hair.

At that moment, he was overwhelmed with emotion, knowing the faith she seemed to have in him. He was her protector, and she trusted him. They had entered into a new version of themselves.

He slid down onto the floor with her, cradling her in his arms, slightly rocking.

"Shh. It's okay. Shh."

The puppy came and nipped at her loose hair.

Allison wiped her nose on the back of her sleeve and giggled. Sweeping the hyper pup into her arms and letting him lick her face, jawline, and down her neck.

Leo looked at him and said jokingly,

"You lucky dog."

"That's what we will call him." She said in between the onslaught of wet kisses.

"We will call him Lucky."

"Lucky it is then." Leo answered.

He repeated "lucky" again as he kissed the top of her head. But it came out sounding exactly how he felt: doubtful.

Everything had gone too easily, and he didn't trust it.

***

Later that night, they laid together on their pallet in front of the fire. Neither of them was able to sleep. She was going over in her mind the fact that she, for all intents and purposes, no longer existed, and he was obsessively replaying the last day's events. They stayed silent.

Allison's whole right side draped over Leo's body, her hand twirling a ringlet of his hair that had found its way to her fingers, while his free hand rubbed her arm. He loved the feel of her skin. It seemed like silk, and he never got bored of it.

He stopped and rolled over to face her. With the light from the fire illuminating her, he focused on her eyes.

Not knowing what to expect, she propped her head up on her elbow and prepared herself to hear the words he was about to say. Knowing they would be important.

"Listen." He began as he moved his hand along her cheek, securing her hair behind her ear.

"We have to make some choices. Your Audi should be discovered pretty quickly. You are still making headlines, so I suspect it won't take long at all. But Allison, it will take the coroner no less than three weeks to decide if they accept that it is in fact you that was in that trunk. We have to be prepared for both outcomes."

"Either way, we will be on the run for the rest of our lives. Do you understand?"

"Yes. I think so."

"What I mean is that we need to get out of here. Out of the cabin, out of the state, out of the *country.*"

"How? How can we do that? My passport is in my safe-deposit box, and...

He sternly stopped her mid-sentence.

"You can't ever use that identity again. *Ever. Do you understand?*"

"If these people find out that I've not done what I was hired to do, if they even suspect that you are still alive, we are all dead. I will be hunted and killed on principle alone. My family would most likely be tortured and murdered, as well as anyone you are close to. As of yesterday, *there is no* Allison Parker."

It was not just the first time she was hearing the words, but the first time she was actually absorbing them. She began to understand exactly what it meant.

She no longer had anything. Home, family, money, identity—nothing. None of what normally defines a person's life. It was all gone. All that she had was the man in front of her, a change of clothes in the form of a workout suit, and her life.

She sat up and hugged her knees. The cold air nipped at her back, and she shivered.

Leo sat up behind her, placing his head just over her shoulder, resting a bit in her hair, his breath on her neck.

"What do we do now? What is going to happen?"

"I will go into the city next week and check to be sure 'you' have been found. I'll pick up the cash drop for my services. I have a friend who makes fake passports. I've already set him in motion for them. We will have temporary finger and palm prints that wear like skin, and they should get us through the international airports and border agents. We will both need to make some changes to our appearance, but from there,

I simply don't know."

"I don't have a plan past getting us as far away from here as possible."

It was finally occurring to her that, as rich as she was, it did her absolutely no good. Dead women don't need cash, and she certainly couldn't just waltz into a bank and pull some out. Not as herself, and not her money, ever again.

It made her head swim.

So lost in her thoughts was she that it went unnoticed when his lips were making their way down her neck and shoulder, only pausing long enough to play with her earlobe with his teeth. His hand was already cupping her breast when she became aware of his wanting.

She tilted her head back and leaned against him. His hand slid down the middle of her stomach, past her belly button, and to the top of her panties.

Anything else that previously occupied her mind was gone, and she allowed her knees to relax and open completely.

He whispered in a low growl,

"Butterfly." Referring to the position of her legs.

She gasped as he inserted two fingers into her, sweeping slowly in an upward motion. As she started to grind against them, he stated rather firmly,

"No. Do not move."

The words alone were enough to send her over the edge, but she did as he asked.

She adored letting him do what he wanted to her, with instructions. It would always play out later in her mind and her dreams.

She tried to resist moving, but he made it impossible. She seemed to have lost control of her own body. It was going to move with or without her decision to stay put or his order to do so.

He stopped, withdrew his fingers, and sucked on them.

Grinning and flushed, he patted her on her right hip a few times; he didn't need to verbalize that command. She knew immediately and leaned forward until she was on her knees in front of him.

She felt his palm across her shoulder blades, pushing. Pushing her down until her shoulders and head were on the floor and her ass was in the air. He slid her panties down to her knees.

"Good girl." He moaned as he put himself inside of her.

Slowly; too slowly. He was toying with her.

She whispered,

"Please."

"Allison. Say it again, louder."

"Please."

"Are you sure?"

She didn't have to see his face to know he was smiling.

"Yes, *oh my God*, yes. *Please.*"

Never before had she wanted anything or anyone as much as she wanted him. She slipped her hand down between her own legs. Teetering on the edge for that long was making her insane.

"Not yet. Just a few more minutes." He told her.

But she wasn't listening. She needed to cum. She *needed* the release more than she had ever needed anything in her life. And even after he stopped moving, she ignored him and kept heading to the edge of that cliff.

He gave into her, picking up tempo and letting her have it. It only took him another minute to follow, and when it was over, he laid on her back. Kissing the soft fleshy part of her neck and shoulder blade.

There would be no more talking that night, but as Allison drifted off to sleep, it dawned on her that she had plenty of cash in this country, in the form of gold Combi bars. The problem was that they were tucked away at Ben's house. The truth was that he probably didn't know what was in the case he'd agreed to store in his safe. But how to get them?

She decided to wait and tell Leo the next morning, and with Lucky curled up at their feet, they slept. Leaving all of the worries for another day.

Fifteen

If it were still 1940s America, Monique would be what would be described as a "traffic stopper."

Slightly above average in height, petite, and thin-framed with curves in all of the right places. Olive complexion, heart-shaped face, and perfectly coiffed chestnut hair that hung just below her shoulder blades.

She had an inner strength that shone even in the way she walked. Something about the way she carried herself demanded attention, and not just from the opposite sex.

From the minute she stepped into a room, people seemed to be at her service.

She was living, breathing, and undeniable proof of "pretty privilege."

She'd probably never had to open a door to an establishment or even hail a cab for herself and had somehow made it to twenty-six years old without ever having or needing a job. She had sex appeal in spades.

And yet, there was something else. Something innocent and childlike.

Maybe it was her almond-shaped brown eyes that made her look more like a baby animal—a doe caught in a storm.

Anyway, there was no shortage of people trying to help or rescue the damsel in distress. Even when there was no distress.

So, when she walked into the police station that day dressed to the nines in her form-fitting knee-length white dress, heels, Burberry coat, and cream-colored Chanel over her shoulder, it was no surprise that she got an immediate and borderline embarrassing welcome.

Two uniformed officers greeted her, along with a female cop who had been seated there initially, followed by a curious detective with a file still in his hand.

She was used to the attention and didn't skip a beat.

"Yes, hello. I need to speak to the detective in charge of the Parker case."

No one spoke. She looked at each one in turn. Awkward silence. She repeated herself slower, assuming they didn't understand through her thick accent.

"The Allison Parker case. I need to speak to the detective in charge of it."

The female police officer sat peering over her glasses and started to speak, but Monique was frustrated and began again, louder. She needed it over with before she changed her mind.

"The missing woman! ALLISON PARKER! I HAVE *INFORMATION. Can I speak to the detective?"*

Female officer,

"Your name?"

She had a piece of paper in her hand, a small form of some kind. She looked up to Monique and repeated herself.

"Your name?"

The four officers all suspiciously stared at her, along with everyone else in the office within earshot, and it made her uncomfortable. It was the wrong kind of attention. She felt her face flush as she answered.

Monique Laurent. L-A-U-R-E-N-T.

The taller, thicker of the officers told her to have a seat in the waiting area. Which she did.

She heard the woman tell one of them to call a detective by the name of Williams. The officer holding the file came from around the counter to ask if she wanted coffee. She declined.

Even after she was seated, the little group didn't disperse. The three stood, their backs turned, speaking in whispers.

Monique settled in for what ended up being a

much longer wait than anticipated.

What she had to tell them kept playing out in her mind. Worded in different ways. She sat and reviewed whole sentences, silently translating them, to assure that when the time came, she wouldn't struggle.

Although she spoke perfect English, from past experience she knew that when she became upset, angry, or nervous, her words tended to come out differently. Jumbled and mixed with French, Italian, and English that sometimes left her confused at her own meaning. She was rooted to the seat by the weight of what she was about to do.

A few feet from her hung an old round clock on the wall. As busy as the room was with activity, she could still hear it. With each second, the long black needle moved into its new position: tick, tick, tick. She zoned in on it and watched it.

It reminded her of school days, hearing each tick while they waited for recess, lunch, or the minute they could leave the building and enjoy the rest of their day doing better things. It was the exact same clock. In every classroom or public office she'd ever been in, but that day it seemed louder somehow.

After an hour, she became restless, and adjusting her purse strap across her shoulder, she got up to leave.

And then a man stood before her.

She hadn't even noticed his approach. One minute he wasn't there, and then he was.

He looked tired. He extended his right hand as he introduced himself, mispronouncing her last name.

"Miss *Lauren,* I'm detective Shultz."

Monique didn't bother correcting him. She absentmindedly shook his hand, looking around him, past him, actively seeking an escape route. The last few minutes before he arrived, she had convinced herself to abort her original plan.

"I'm sorry, I've made a mistake." She said and turned to leave.

She was almost to the elevator when he called out to her.

"Miss, you can either come back and share the information you have, or we can tail you until we find out for ourselves. You've probably already put yourself in danger just by coming here, and withholding information makes you an accomplice. Do you know what that means? It means you will be held accountable the same as if you'd done it. At least let us protect you from whatever it is you are afraid of. If you have anything that would help us, please reconsider."

Shultz didn't know who she was or what she knew, but he did know that she was the first bit of a light at the end of the tunnel he'd had in the case. They were out of leads and had spent weeks rehashing old information. He couldn't let her walk out the door easily. He had a hunch whatever she had to say was worth hearing. Giving up before he even had a chance to question her was not an option.

Elevator button pushed, Monique stood in front of it and waited. The doors opened, but her feet wouldn't move from the spot.

When they closed, she turned to face the detective.

"I'm not afraid."

"Okay, then what would be the harm in talking?"

She relented.

Too aware of her high heels clicking on the tile floor, she followed him to another room. Everyone and everything seemed to have stopped.

She scanned the area, and it was as if someone had pushed pause. They all watched her. She ducked her head down a little and continued walking. Almost running into Shultz when he stopped just inside the hallway in front of an unmarked room.

He held the door open ahead of her and nodded toward a chair on the other side of a table.

It was without a doubt the most sterile room she had ever been in. She took her seat, more uncomfortable than ever. She was in a corner, proverbially and literally, and there was no backing out.

Shultz had a seat opposite her. He had a legal pad in front of him, his hands clasped together on top of it.

After the expected pleasantries that included an offer of a beverage, a comment about the weather, and an inquiry as to what part of France she was from, he casually asked her "what he could do for her."

The interview had begun.

He had eased from one personality to the other so smoothly she hadn't even noticed the transition. At least until she felt her throat constrict. Her resolve wasn't shaken, but she still struggled in the beginning.

It wasn't like she hadn't betrayed a man's trust before, but that time seemed different somehow. It wasn't for integrity or even manipulation. It was completely for monetary gain.

She desperately needed something, and the

only way to get it was to betray the only man she'd ever loved.

She knew she should be confessing what she knew because it was the right thing morally, but that wasn't the reason at all, making her feel twice as guilty. The fact was that her morals had gone out the window years ago. She never would have survived otherwise.

No matter how innocent she appeared, she wasn't naive—something that both she *and* the detective knew.

She cleared her throat, and more matter-of-factly than she had dreamed possible, she told him.

"You are right. I am risking a lot to come here. What will I get in return?"

Shultz squinted his eyes and immediately understood. He didn't say anything at first but considered the new condition as it was introduced to the situation.

"I know that large cash rewards are normally given for information."

"Well," Shultz said, "that really depends on the information."

"You are going to want to hear what I have to say, detective."

He never broke eye contact and asked,

"I can't and won't promise anything until you give me insight on *who* you are and how you even tie into all of this. You're going to have to give me something to go on—respectfully."

Monique shifted in her chair, then dug in her handbag for a moment before pulling out a silver cigarette case. The likes of which he hadn't seen since he was a small boy. She was a paradox. Floating somewhere in between young and beautiful and born in a century past.

"Do you mind?" she asked.

If he did mind, it wouldn't have mattered; it was already lit.

They didn't normally allow smoking in the building, but he wasn't going to do anything that would deny her comfort. He stood and yelled out the door to someone she couldn't see to bring him something to be used as an ashtray, then took his seat again.

Her left arm was folded across the table; she held the cigarette in between her index and middle fingers while rubbing her thumb and pinkie together.

She was studying him, sizing him up. The roles seemed to have reversed from the minute she started smoking.

As she exhaled a cloud through her nostrils and mouth, she said,

"For the last year, I have been Heath Parker's lover. I still am."

The door opened. A uniformed officer placed an old foil ashtray on the table beside her, then left as quickly as he'd come in.

Shultz's eyes never left her, but he didn't say anything. He was too stunned. There was no way in hell they had missed one of Heath's lovers. Especially one that looked like her. He was more than a little skeptical.

He habitually patted himself down, feeling for his own pack of Winstons, quickly realizing he only carried them when he left the building for breaks or lunch.

Monique slid the silver case across the table. He took one between his teeth and again searched himself—that time for a lighter. She handed him hers.

He hadn't smoked inside of the precinct in over fifteen years, but it didn't feel out of the ordinary. It actually felt normal for some odd reason.

"I'm going to need more, Miss Lauren."

Monique saw the doubt in his eyes, or maybe it was confusion. She had done a great job those last months staying off the radar and out of the line of fire. Her mind went through what she had that would prove to him she was telling the truth. But she needed to have the monetary deal settled before she got too elaborate.

"Before I say too much, I need an assurance that I won't be held. I am coming here of my own free will. Surely that counts for something."

Shultz took a drag while deciding on his next words.

"I can't promise that. Not until I know the details and you are obviously here for the money, not as a good Samaritan."

He prematurely snubbed his cigarette out and said,

"So why don't you tell me why I should believe that out of dozens of women we have found, contacted, and interviewed in the last few weeks, not once has your name come up. I have never seen or heard of you, and it's my job. And I am good at my job, Miss Lauren."

Something in the way he expressed himself. He had a way of calling her a liar without actually saying the word, and it affected Monique in an unexpected way. Like a sixteen-year-old kid being accused of something they absolutely *did* do. Pride alone was enough for her to feel the need to prove herself. Did she look like someone who would make up a reason to get involved in a kidnapping?

She reached into her coat pocket and pulled

out a small flip phone. The ones people stopped using when smartphones hit the market.

She opened her smartphone, touched some buttons, and slid it across the table in his direction.

While he read the message, she explained.

"Heath has one; I have one. We do not communicate any other way. We haven't for almost a year. At first, I didn't know why. Later, when I found out, it was too late. I already loved him."

She pulled out her modern cell phone, tapped on the screen a few times, and turned it around for the detective to see.

It was a photo of her and a Heath; he appeared to be asleep. It was time- and date-stamped.

Shultz took it from her and stared at it. The picture was taken just after Mrs. Parker had been abducted.

"I have more. More pictures, more messages, and more information. You are running out of time. *She* is running out of time, and so is her son."

She paused for effect before saying his name.

"Ben."

She reached into her coat pocket and said,

"I received this right after she disappeared."

She slid a folded piece of paper across the table to him. He unfolded and read it. In block letters it simply read:

I KNOW WHO YOU ARE—AND I KNOW THAT YOU KNOW.

It was enough.

He looked up to the left corner of the room, where a video camera was installed. Before saying,

"What is it you want, Miss Lauren?"

Without hesitation, she replied.

"I need to know I will be safe. Safe from prosecution and safe from the people involved. I could disappear as easily as she did. I need enough money to go home. I want to go back to France as soon as possible. I will agree to tell you everything I know and testify, but without Heath, I have no way to live or support myself. I need the reward."

"Miss Lauren, are you implying that Heath Parker is responsible for the disappearance of Mrs. Parker?"

She sat back in her chair, resolved. Curt in her reply.

"I will not say another word until we have an agreement. *In writing.*"

Shultz excused himself. He got up, left the room, and closed the door behind him. Leaning on it for a minute, he had to calm his thoughts. He was overwhelmed. The case had consumed his life for weeks, and the answer just waltzed into the precinct on a random Tuesday. It was almost too much to take.

He gathered his wits, called Williams, and told him to come immediately. He let Monique sit by herself smoking cigarettes while he made a strategy plan. After a quick meeting with the chief, he collected the necessary paperwork. He didn't need her feet getting cold.

Order of protection, affidavit, consent for interview, conditions of the reward—they all had to be presented and filled out. He retrieved the thick PARKER abduction file, and since his partner hadn't made it back to the office yet, he requested that officer Pierce join him.

Anytime he felt a case was about to be solved, the excitement gave him a rush, but that day it made him a bit sick to his stomach. He took an acid reducer, chased it with water, and headed back in to join Miss Laurent.

"Ellen!" He yelled out to the female officer, "Can you bring in a cup of tea? There's some Earl Grey in my office."

His phone rang. It was Detective Williams on the other end. Shultz assumed he was calling to let him know when he would make it.

"Yeah, I'm heading into the interview room now. How far away are you?"

Williams,

"I just got word from a friend of mine, a sheriff over in Clark County. Parker's torched Audi was found near an old landfill a few miles from the Hood River."

Shultz stood with his phone propped between his neck and cheek. He put the paperwork under his armpit and grasped the phone in his hand but didn't respond.

His partner's words had stopped him dead in his tracks.

"Dave, what could possibly be the remains of a body were in the trunk."

Before Shultz had time to digest the new information, he looked up to see Ben Parker coming out of the elevator.

"For fuck's sake."

Sixteen

Ben had never held a gun in his hands and, in fact, couldn't recall one time in his life that he had even been in the same room with one, omitting the occasions he had been around a police officer or standing in line at the bank, of course.

The weapon felt heavier, but otherwise, just as he'd imagined it whenever he had watched an actor or actress fire one off into a villain. It was odd to him that before he had even held it, he understood exactly how it would feel. Somehow, he just knew. The same way he would know how it would feel to lick the pavement or a pillow, or anything for that matter. His brain just filled in the unknown experience with its own very accurate detail.

Holding it felt wrong but also so very powerful.

Jake took the revolver from his hand and gave it back to the salesman behind the counter. He had previous experience with weapons from his short stint in the Army reserves and handled them the way one would with experience.

He handed Ben a smaller one. It felt less awkward.

"Try this one; it's a Ruger 9mm. It might be more comfortable for you since you have smaller hands."

Ben grasped it firmly, and doing what everyone probably does the first time they hold a weapon; he placed his index finger on the trigger.

"No, *no, Ben*!"

Jake's words came out harsher than he'd intended. He placed his hand on top of the gun, pushing the barrel down.

"Benjamin, do not ever put your finger on the trigger of a gun until you have aimed and are ready to fire, and never point a gun anywhere except the floor or an intentional target. Both are bad habits, ones that cause accidents."

"Look, like this."

Jake took the weapon, showing him the proper way to hold it while giving him a quick tutorial on where the safety lever was and where to place the stock.

The man behind the counter stood watching, randomly telling them features of that particular model. None of which he understood.

Ben stood with it, listening to both give him

instructions on how to do this or that. He felt overwhelmed. He lowered the weapon and placed it onto the counter, then shoved his hands into his jacket pockets, obviously uncomfortable.

As he turned away from the display case, Jake put his hand on his shoulder to prevent him from walking away. He leaned in and said in a low voice,

"Babe, I know this feels a bit drastic to you. I understand it goes against everything you've ever believed in, but trust me when I say it is the right thing to do given the circumstances. *We have no choice.* You'll probably never have to use it, but it's better to be safe than sorry. Just buy one, let me teach you how to use it, and that way you will at least be prepared. I am not always home, you know."

Coming from Jake, it made more sense to him than if it would have come from anyone else. Normally being the passionate part of their duo, he still said the words with conviction instead of fear.

Ben considered the facts again. His mother's Audi had been found a few weeks prior, and they were waiting on confirmation that it was, in fact, her body in the trunk. It just so happened that they had received the news on his birthday, and he seemed to be the only one to have doubts. At any time, they expected the news that would make him the sole heir to her fortune and simultaneously the prime target.

And if his father had anything to do with it, as he suspected, he was the only person standing in the way. He didn't feel like he had a choice in the matter; he needed to be able to protect himself.

Jake didn't share his suspicions about Heath, but after the note found in their house and Ben's early intuition on the matter, it was enough to make him extra cautious—enough to be at a gun store shopping for a weapon.

After a few minutes of consideration, Ben turned back to the counter and picked the handgun up again.

"This one feels good."

Resolved, he said, "Yeah, this one."

Jake told the salesman,

"We'll take the Ruger and two boxes of bullets, please.

Three hours later, they were at a gun range.

It didn't take much time or teaching for Ben to get the hang of it. Jake was impressed. It appeared that Ben was a natural marksman.

***

They left the range and stopped off to have a

bite, so it was late evening when they returned home.

As they pulled into the driveway, they saw Heath's car parked on the street.

He was sitting on their top front step, elbows on his knees, beer in his hand. Which struck Jake in an odd way. It was frigid outside.

The fact he wasn't *on* the porch in one of the three chairs or the swing just acknowledged the space between them, a visual representation of the coldness, distance, and unfamiliarity he and Ben shared.

Ben groaned, "What the hell is he doing here?"

Jake turned the car off, reached over, and squeezed his hand before taking the gun and putting it into their "doggie bag" from the restaurant. He had already reloaded the magazine before leaving the range and put the box of shells into the glove box.

Jake sighed, "I don't know; let's go see."

With a little more than dread from both of them, they got out and approached the porch.

Heath didn't bother getting up until both men were at the door. He retrieved a bag of his own from one of the chairs and followed them into the house.

The awkwardness was inordinate. No greetings, handshakes, or affectionate gestures. It was tense, to say the least.

Once inside, Heath placed what remained of a six-pack of Stella into their refrigerator and two bottles of wine on the counter. He trashed his empty beer and popped the top on a new one. He opened several cabinets until he located the wine glasses, retrieving two and placing them on the island. And all of this was done without a word. You could cut the air with a knife.

Jake broke the silence first, telling Ben,

"I have to go to the gallery for a few hours." Then, in a lower voice,

"Are you going to be okay?"

Ben glanced over to his father, who had filled a glass presumably for him with his favorite red; he then left the second one empty. He headed to the den situated right beside the kitchen and placed the glass on the coffee table in between the two sofas and removed his coat.

"Yes, I'll be fine. Thank you for taking the day off; I never would have done it without you."

Knowing that outward signs of affection in front of his father weren't acceptable, Jake reached over, placed his hand on Ben's shoulder, and squeezed, expressing his support. He put the leftovers from dinner into the fridge, and being out of view of their visitor, he removed the gun and tucked it into a utility drawer in their island.

With one last pat on the shoulder, he tilted his chin up to acknowledge Heath, who had installed himself on their couch, and left.

Ben watched him go and then turned his attention to his father. He was leaning back, one arm stretched across the back of the sofa, the other hand holding a beer. His knees were relaxed and spread wide, like a slouch. He looked so out of place, and his presence in the room felt like a direct violation of all that is fine and classy. To put it simply, he marred the beautiful surroundings. Like a dirty speck on white linen.

Space that had been tailor-made to feel simply elegant and homey felt chaotic and ugly with him in it. His father carried a cloud around with him—his own personal dark aura that affected any space he occupied, especially the space he was currently in.

It seemed to Jake that the only reason he was ever tolerable was that his mother was with him. He realized he had never really spent any time alone with his father and that his mother's presence usually made his dad all but invisible. She was the sole reason Ben had ever been able to stomach him, and she wasn't there.

He watched as Heath leaned forward and removed his loafers, then crossed his leg into a position to rub his socked foot.

He went into the den and sat on the couch opposite him. He still had no idea why he was there. But any interest in finding out was feigned; he didn't really care.

Heath took a big swig of beer before asking,

"How's your catering business going, son?"

Ben stared at him for a moment. His father's presence made him uneasy and annoyed.

"Cut the crap, Dad. I know you didn't come to ask about my business, or to check on me for that matter; we both know you don't give a shit about either."

Heath leaned forward and put his beer on the table between them. He interlaced his fingers and looked down. His shoulders slack, his demeanor unreadable.

"You're so much like your mother."

There was a bite in his remark.

He sighed and leaned back again, the buttons midway down his shirt struggling against the extra weight around his belly.

Ben became even more agitated than normal and realized it probably had to do with the fact his father was in a rare state; he was sober.

Usually by that time of day he was drunk. Ben knew how to handle an intoxicated Heath but was in unfamiliar territory with the version in front of him.

"Look, Ben. I know our relationship has been strained, but..."

He stopped as if trying to hold back emotion. Emotion that Ben knew he didn't have.

"I wasn't going to come by. To be completely honest, I've been avoiding you for weeks, unsure of what to say or how to console you. But I realized these last few days that you and I are all that we have left. No matter what, you are still my son. Whether you believe me or not, I miss her too."

Heath's eyes began to glaze over, and he thought he saw a trickle of sincerity in him—real concern. For the first time, he felt empathy for his father.

"I just needed to come have a drink and spend some time with my son; is that so wrong?"

Ben shrugged and focused his attention on a painting on the wall directly above his father's head. It was one of his mother's first efforts of him and Trixie. A pattern she would repeat every few years. She'd updated them as he grew, but that one he was especially fond of. It brought him solace just to look at it.

After a long pause, "No, dad, I suppose not."

Heath leaned in and grabbed his beer, stretching his arm across the table and tilting the neck of the bottle towards Ben's untouched wine. A sign for him to drink.

Ben picked up the glass, raising it high for a second before putting it to his lips. He leaned back, holding it in his lap. The first nervous gulp had been a welcome one.

They talked for a bit about work, Jake, and a few other mundane topics, but not one word was spoken about Allison. The proverbial elephant in the room.

It was as if they were catching up on all of the details of Ben's life that Heath had missed. It felt pleasing that he seemed to be genuinely interested, and it occurred to Ben that maybe he had been wrong about him.

For the first time in their lives, they were getting along. Lulling him into a false sense of security.

"I am sorry, son; I am truly sorry for everything."

The words he had waited to hear his whole life, and there they were.

But he couldn't absorb them. They echoed through his mind, pinging back and forth like a tennis ball in a concrete box—only the box was his head.

He looked through blurred vision at the empty sofa across from him. Where was his father?

The glass in his hand had tilted over, and he looked down to see what remained of the red wine spilling down the sea-foam green fabric. He was aware of it; he saw it but could no longer grasp the glass. His arms limp at his side, his head bogged down and unable to move. He could only observe, not respond.

He heard his father's words as if underwater.

"I *really am sorry, Ben.*"

And then—sleep.

Seventeen

Leo made it into Ben's house for the second time. He followed Allison's instruction and found the safe with no issue. It was the old-fashioned type with a rolling dial. After trying several times with the combination she'd shared, he couldn't get it open. He was frustrated and about to give up when he decided to start the sequence of numbers counterclockwise, and it worked.

He was in the office just off of the kitchen when he heard a car door slam. He peered out the window and saw Heath. He gathered up the gold micro-bars and a few velvet boxes of jewelry and put them into his backpack, then quietly closed the safe and stood by the door considering his options.

He had come in the French doors on the other side of the den, but he wasn't sure if there was a way out of the backyard without going down the side of the house and through the front yard. And he knew from experience the gate would be locked. He'd climbed the fence from the alley earlier but didn't have the time to exit the same way without being seen.

A few minutes into his dilemma, he heard two more car doors slam. Again, he looked out the window and saw Ben and Jake arrive. *Fuck.*

Positioning himself behind the partially open door, he saw the three men enter. He was trapped.

He watched the scene play out before him, at some point almost forgetting he was an intruder. He found himself too close to the doorjamb and eased back to stifle a sneeze, returning just in time to see Ben's partner put a gun in the drawer—intentionally out of sight of their guest.

He felt his own head nod in silent approval; smart guy.

He heard Jake leave and turned his attention to Heath.

He loathed the man, and not just because of Allison. He had a distaste for anyone who displayed greed, disloyalty, or sneaky behavior, and that man had been all of those things—not only to the woman he now loved but also to his own son. Leo started to get worked up and felt a trickle of sweat roll down the side of his face, his hands moist and hot inside the latex gloves.

He felt in his core that something was off.

In all of the months he had followed Allison and watched Heath and their family life, he'd not once seen Heath treat his boy with even a hint of respect or kindness, and there he was, doing just that.

Leo listened for a while as they talked. Trying to get insight on why Heath had all of a sudden changed.

He heard him ask Ben questions—ones that should convey a feeling of affection or care. He observed as Ben became more relaxed and less bitter in his answers and demeanor, all the while knowing that whatever was going on was certainly *not* a father-son bonding moment. He felt real fear for the young man, and after almost an hour of watching their exchange, he understood why.

His intuition was spot-on.

At some point, Ben's words became garbled, his responses slower. He was having trouble putting words together at all, and Leo just knew.

And then, Ben sat slouched to the side of the couch, resting on the arm, his glass laid across his lap.

Unsure of what to do, Leo stayed where he was.

Heath put his shoes on and went to the kitchen. He emptied the remainder of the open bottle. Then he opened the second, poured out over half of its contents, and placed it on the counter. He walked over to the stove and turned the knobs, opening the valve on all four burners without igniting them. He put his coat on, grabbed keys from a basket, and went out the back door. The side gate hinges squeaked.

Leo was just about to make a move when he heard two men speaking. They were right outside the window of the office, but he couldn't make out what they were saying.

Heath returned moments later, dropped the keys, grabbed the empty bottle of wine, and without even turning back around, left out the front door.

Still unsure if it was safe, Leo remained behind the door, peeking into the kitchen and den, waiting. Another ten minutes went by as the smell of gas filled the room. And then he saw what he'd already anticipated—Heath was a coward and was incapable of doing his own dirty work—that he was positive of.

An unknown man came in through the French doors. He stood just inside, surveying the area. He had a mask over his mouth and nose and gloves similar to the ones Leo was wearing. He looked right at the office door, directly at Leo, as if he knew. Neither of them moved a muscle.

The man crossed the den, all but ignored Ben and headed straight toward him.

But then, he stopped. He wasn't headed for

him, but the utility closet just beside the kitchen instead.

Leo let out a sigh of relief. He couldn't see the man anymore and wondered exactly what he was doing. He heard a door open, and what sounded like a heavy wrench fall onto tile. And then he understood. He was in the water heater closet. He was dismantling the gas tube.

When the man appeared again, he walked over to the small fireplace in the corner and turned the switch on. He stopped and stood, hovering over Ben for a minute as if contemplating something.

Reaching down, he pushed Ben over just enough to retrieve his wallet from his back pocket. He thumbed through it, pulled out the cash, shoved it into his front pocket, and threw the wallet onto Ben's lap.

Leo watched as the man pulled a bottle of lighter fluid out of his jacket pocket and saturated a rag, then poured the rest on and around Ben. He was reaching into his pocket again, and Leo didn't need to see any more to know what he was about to do. He had to take quick action.

Without giving the unknown assailant time to react, he flew from behind the protection of the door. In one quick movement, he grabbed the gun from the drawer and charged him. Leo, without hesitation, released the safety, and fired two shots directly into the man's head at point-blank range.

The shots echoed in the small room.

His ears ringing, he dropped the weapon and ran from the house. Across the backyard and over the fence in record time. He didn't stop. He was down the alley and into his Jeep four blocks over in a matter of minutes.

He started the engine and sped away.

Before he could even catch his breath or get out of the subdivision, he heard sirens. As he fled down the main road toward the highway, he passed several police cars and ambulances heading in the opposite direction and knew Ben was going to be okay.

***

Detective Shultz and Williams sat in an unmarked van a few houses down from Ben's.

Even with all of the information Monique had given them, they still needed more. She had no actual proof or details, just hearsay. She could be written off as a scorned lover. Not having the coroner's decision yet, there was little they could do except watch and wait. They had officers watching Ben as well as Heath around the clock, but that particular day Shultz and Williams were tailing Heath and were surprised to see him pay a visit to his son.

Shultz was eating leftovers from Tupperware while Williams was having a burger they picked up on the way to their shift. They were sharing cold fries from a bag between them when they observed Heath get into his car and leave.

They were going to finish eating and send the second team to follow Heath. Swapping positions for a while. They were pretty sure he was going to end up at a pub for the next few hours anyway. What did it matter which officers were sitting in a parking lot somewhere while he did?

They had barely finished their food, and Shultz was smoking a cigarette when they heard the shots. They knew immediately where they'd come from.

Williams called for backup as they rushed to the door. After pounding a few times and ringing the doorbell, Williams yelled out,

"POLICE! MR. PARKER, OPEN THE DOOR!"

They were met with silence. The door was locked, and even from outside, the smell of propane was overwhelming.

Guns drawn, they made their way around the side of the house, entering the backyard through the open gate. The double doors were swinging; the curtains blew in the breeze. They approached cautiously, calling Ben's name.

Slowly, Shultz pushed the door inward.

A few feet inside on the floor, a man laid sprawled face up—blood freely flowing from an obvious gunshot wound. The maroon circle around his head was growing larger by the minute, thick and dark on the plush area rug. A gun visible just inches away.

Gas permeated the small space, and the detectives covered their noses and mouths with the crooks of their arms.

Williams checked on Ben while Shulz ran over and shut off the valves on the stove. He knew that couldn't be the only source.

After realizing Ben was alive, they picked him up from either side, propping his arms up over their shoulders; they half carried and half dragged him out of there.

The ambulance arrived just as they made their way to the front of the house. It was apparent that someone had called 911 first.

Detective Shultz rode with him to the hospital while Williams stayed behind and waited for the gas company and the forensic team. It was going to be a long night.

Eighteen

Ben woke up in the hospital. Jake held his hand while Shultz sat in a chair in the corner. They had been there for almost eighteen hours—plenty of time for toxicology test results.

Ben had enough Halcion and Ketamine in him to knock out a horse. He was lucky to be alive.

Jake had filled in the officer on everything he could from the day before. The gun store, shooting range, and, of course, Heath's visit. All of which he already knew.

They had adequate suspicion and circumstantial evidence for Heath to be in custody, but not enough to detain him for more than 72 hours. The forensic team was doing tests on the wine bottle, and they were still waiting on a warrant to search his residence.

The whole scene had been confusing.

They had no idea who the dead man was or who had shot him. They were waiting on prints to come back; none had yet. As far as they could tell, the unknown male wasn't in their criminal database.

As per protocol, Ben's fingers were swabbed for gunshot residue, but it was pointless. They knew he had fired a weapon that day, several times, and other than the gun shop employee, he and Jake's prints were the only ones found on the weapon.

They also knew Ben had to have been too incapacitated to be the shooter, and the shots were fired *after* Heath left. There were no signs of forced entry or anything taken. The only plausible explanation being that Heath had let the intruder in.

They were left with more questions than answers, and it was frustrating.

***

Ben was released from the hospital the next morning. Their home was still a crime scene, and they were supposed to go to a hotel for a few days until they were told otherwise. Ben decided to make a detour.

He wanted to go to his parents' house. He had to be in his mother's space for a while. Just to see her things and be somewhere that he felt a connection.

As they pulled onto Poppy Lane, they knew immediately something was up.

Police cars, forensic vans, and television crews lined the street. They couldn't get closer than ten houses down. Jake inched the car through the maze of obstacles close enough for Ben to get out and make a run for the door. His parent's neighbors and onlookers all stood in a cluster near the edge of the yard. Cameras were everywhere, and questions were being shouted out to him. Questions he had no intention of answering.

When he made it to the porch, a uniformed police officer tried to stop him.

"I'm Ben Parker. What's going on?"

Just as he asked the question, Shultz saw him and waved to the officer to let him in.

"Our warrant came through. You have a right to be here, Mr. Parker, but stay out of the way. If we need anything, I'll ask. Otherwise, just let us do our job."

Ben nodded his agreement.

He watched as officers searched, not really understanding what it was they were looking for. But he had no doubt left that his father was behind all of it, and he hoped they would find whatever they needed to ensure he stayed locked up. It was the only way he felt safe.

In an effort to make himself invisible, he wandered into the only room in the house he wished to go—his mom's art studio.

He went in and half closed the door behind him. He always felt connected to her in that room.

Sitting in a chair, he stared at her last incomplete project. Another picture of him and Trixie. The paint had dried completely in those weeks, and he reached up to touch the raised strokes. Her use of texture was fascinating. Something her paintings always had. He loved the way she added depth to her art that way. It was something that set hers apart from others.

Trixie's fur should feel soft; it looked soft. He traced her outline.

Tears rolled down his face as he picked up one of his mother's brushes. He leaned back and twirled it between his fingers. Just a few weeks earlier, she had held it. He ran his palm across the soft sable and then brought it to his nose to breathe in the smell he loved so much. Familiarity. Comfort. It smelled like home—like her.

He placed the brush back into the holder and walked around the room a bit. Running his hands along surfaces, touching everything. Anything that her energy was attached to. He wasn't thinking really; he was just roaming around the room, taking it all in.

He spotted her leather-bound black sketchbook on a shelf. He grabbed it and took a seat again, laying it out on the desk. As he thumbed through it, he was reminded of how good she really was. Each picture, although rough, displayed a perfect style; details were amazing, and even her drawing of a bird looked as if it could fly from the page. He smiled to himself.

Ben enjoyed the book and lingered over each sketch unhurried.

As he got to the last page, he was about to close it and return it to the shelf when he found an envelope tucked tightly against the binding.

Curious, he flipped it over.

In his mother's handwriting, *~BENJAMIN* was printed across the front. His heart fluttered as he opened the unsealed letter.

He inhaled deeply, exhaled, and read:

Ben,

If you are reading this letter, it means I am gone. It means that I didn't make it out soon enough, and your father has succeeded in killing me.

Benjamin; I have been followed these last months. I've observed on numerous occasions a man stalking me. Everywhere I go. The market, the gym, the park—he is always there.

At first, I thought I was being paranoid, but if you are reading this letter now, it is proof I was correct. The most important thing to tell you is simply this:

You have been the light of my life, and I am so damn proud of the man you have become. You are everything your father is not. Everything I hoped for in a child. Everything I dreamed of. Everything I expected.

I have left everything to you. Enjoy your life, and do not let this define your future. You have too much goodness in you to let anything change your direction.

There is a safe. It is in the pool guest house, behind the vanity mirror. All that the authorities will need is in that safe. It is the only thing I can do now.

The digital code is the day we brought Trixie home. Remember?

I Love You Son,

MOM

Ben read the letter three times. His shaking hands made it impossible to read a fourth. He rushed out of the room to go find Shultz.

***

It was Christmas Eve, and Leo hadn't been the same since he'd returned to the cabin a few days earlier. Allison couldn't quite put her finger on it, but something was very different.

He came back with their passports and news that the coroner hadn't made a decision yet. They knew there was the possibility it would take a while, so it really wasn't a surprise. That couldn't be what had him acting so strange.

She knew him well enough to know that he was carrying something heavy—the weight of something great enough to change everything about him.

Subtle things, really. But to her, it was very obvious.

He didn't engage or look her in the eye. Even when they made love, his mind seemed to be elsewhere. There was an invisible wall between them.

She knew better than to ask him questions and believed when he was ready to tell her, he would. So, she waited. Going through the days as if nothing were wrong. Watching him, anticipating the moment when he would free his mind and share whatever darkness had enveloped him.

Allison spent the afternoon roasting chicken

and preparing a few side dishes. More so that she would feel like it was a holiday than anything. It was her first Christmas away from Ben, and she was trying to stave off melancholy of her own.

They sat at the dinner table. Leo picked at his food, and Lucky stood close by, head tilted, staring at them, licking his chops.

"Oh! I've almost forgotten." He said, suddenly rising from the table. "I'll be right back."

He went outside for a few minutes, and when he returned, he had something hidden behind his back.

As he approached, he revealed a bottle of wine, and she couldn't help but smile.

"It is Christmas. I don't know anything about wine, but the man at the store said this would go perfectly with any meal."

Clearly in shock, Allison's mouth was hanging open. He leaned down and kissed her on the lips.

"Merry Christmas."

She watched as he filled two teacups with the burgundy and said,

"I think I'll join you."

Then she *knew* something was wrong. That gesture alone was enough to remove any doubt that he was hiding something.

He took his seat again, placing the open bottle between them. Lucky had given up and laid sleeping beside her chair.

They ate in silence and enjoyed the wine. Allison hadn't had a drink in so long; she had a slight buzz when she cleared the table. As she stacked the dishes in the drain, Leo came up behind her. His arms encircled her waist, and he leaned his head over her shoulder.

"Do that later. Come in here; I have another surprise."

She still had the dish towel in her hand as he led her away from the sink. He had the look of an excited little boy. He told her to sit and cover her eyes.

"What are you up to?" she said, while doing exactly what he asked.

After a few minutes of what sounded like him getting something from the porch, he said, "Okay, you can open them."

Allison opened her eyes. It took her a minute to actually comprehend what was in front of her.

Leo stood, a small canvas in one hand and a wooden box in the other. She knew exactly what it contained. He had brought her paints!

"I have an easel too."

Allison flew from the chair and threw her arms around his neck so quickly he didn't have time to empty his hands. He stood holding onto the objects of her joy and let her kiss him all over his face. Both of them were giggling while Lucky spun around at their feet, barking.

"Whoa, whoa!" Leo crinkled his nose and stepped back, smiling, feigning a coy response to her affectionate attack.

"I've ordered the vanilla linseed oil; until I pick it up, the regular smelly stuff will have to do."

Allison didn't listen or care but absentmindedly remarked,

"I have an allergy."

She took the box, sat down on the floor, and opened it. Brushes, a palette, and a wide range of oil paints. Good ones. She took each color out in turn, reading the tube and saying the names out loud. She was in heaven.

Her joy was infectious; he stood grinning, watching her. So proud that he had provided the cause of happiness she wore plastered across her face.

"Oh Leo, thank you." She said as she pulled the bundle of brushes to her chest.

"You are welcome; the look on your face is all the thanks I need. Merry Christmas, Allison."

The wall was down again, and she forgot that anything had actually changed in him. If only temporarily.

Nineteen

Leo watched her paint for hours. Each stroke deliberate and painstakingly thoughtful. He observed as a plain white canvas received the colors in layers of blue and white, brown and green. Hues of oily cream in darks and lights, until her creation finally took shape. Until the details became an obvious portrait of him.

Against a backdrop of snow-covered ground and a wooded tree line. The only part of her surroundings she had seen for months; the only thing she could draw inspiration from.

She was a wonder to behold. So talented, so beautiful.

She stood wearing one of his flannel button-downs in her panties, her hair held up in a bun with a pencil. Wisps falling around her face and down her neck. He couldn't willfully stop himself from gazing at her.

He watched intently, with equal amounts of lust, fascination, and love. He focused solely on what was in front of him so as not to let in more grim intrusive thoughts. He struggled to accept what he knew to be fact.

For those last few days, the only thing that had occupied his brain, on repeat, was the knowledge that *he had killed a man—he was a murderer.*

And for him, that wasn't the worst part. The scene he kept replaying and trying to understand was the part where he had done it without a second thought. He did it to save a man he didn't even know and did it without one ounce of hesitation. More than that, he really didn't feel guilty about it. It only occupied his brain because he was afraid to tell Allison.

Afraid of what, he didn't know.

Her judgment? The loss of her admiration or care? He was more afraid of losing the faith she had in him—the opinion he had worked so hard to create. He valued it. What if she saw him as a monster?

The longer he kept it to himself, the harder it was to tell, and the worse the outcome would be. That he was sure of.

Saturated with his new memories, he didn't notice when she sighed deeply, put down the brush and palette, and went to the kitchen to wash her hands.

She seemed lost in her own head. As if she had taken a pause from the real world.

It appeared to him that while she was

painting, her mind was free and clear. Calm and peaceful. He didn't want to interrupt that. And so, for hours, he'd stayed silent. An outsider looking in. Just like when he used to watch her from behind her backyard shrubbery, only now he wasn't doing it in secret.

As the day drew to a close, he became more resolved. He decided that he needed to confess. If for no other reason than to give her reassurance that Ben was safe. He had kept her son safe. Surely that would outweigh exactly *what* he had done to keep him that way.

At least that was his hope.

***

Jake stood at the railing overlooking the gallery. Other than holding a paintbrush or charcoaling an outline for a new piece of work, it was his favorite place to be. There was something about standing in the middle between the double staircase with a perfect view of the entrance, the circular main hall, and the front desk that put him at complete ease.

He watched the strangers milling around, taking notice of which artist's work captured their attention long enough for them to shut up. The pieces that needed to be enjoyed with their eyes and weren't discussed at all. Those were the ones that made his job and his life worthwhile.

He leaned over and rested his forearms on the cold, shiny steel banister. Trying to make up his mind on whether to tell Ben or the police about something that was eating at him. Something small; insignificant perhaps—he couldn't decide one way or another.

Two days earlier, an order came across his desk. An order that, under any other circumstance, he wouldn't have thought twice about. But something about the yellow carbon copy with one almost illegible line troubled him: (x2) *Vanilla Linseed Oil.*

It had somehow wormed its way into his head and gotten entangled with his more rational thoughts. It is safe to say Jake was not a conspiracy theorist and didn't buy into anything that went beyond common sense.

But the fact was, he had been an artist for the past twenty years, producing his first painting at seven years old. He was tasked with curating for the last three, and he couldn't remember once in all of that time having anyone come to the gallery and ask for vanilla linseed oil. Although they did offer art classes once a month, they weren't an art supply store and didn't make a habit of selling such things.

There was only one person he knew other than himself that used it or knew that they could get it there: Allison.

He always ordered it from France for his own use and kept a few spares for her.

He stood upright, put his hands on his hips, and rotated his body around. First right, then left. A ritualistic habit he'd acquired at some point in his career when he was stressed or indecisive. Stretch, stretch, breathe in, breathe out.

He went back into his office and picked up the sheet again.

Across the top of the order form, it said "*Oscar.*" No phone number, no address. He folded it and put it into the breast pocket of his jacket. He grabbed his keys and decided to call it a day.

He left the gallery still unsure of what to make of it.

***

Both detectives were exhausted. They had been either at the Parker residence or at the precinct for days. Every other case was handed off to another team; they had their hands full.

They found the safe exactly where Allison's letter said it would be. The forensic team would have found it eventually, but it certainly saved them time and effort. It contained an unbelievable amount of evidence, and they were tirelessly going through it one item at a time.

Carefully bagged and tagged, different departments had bits of it, which left Williams and Shultz to go through the stacks of paperwork and verify each piece of the puzzle she'd left behind.

It appeared that the last year Allison had saved everything.

To include a small bag with Heath's fingerprints with Halcion residue, to more concrete evidence of illegal activities such as insider trading. It contained copies of a new life insurance policy he'd taken out on his wife, as well as video surveillance of their backyard saved on a thumb drive. Every single item made the case against Heath stronger. All roads led to him. There was no denying it.

Allison had left them a gift. Everything they needed to put Heath away for life—wrapped up with a neat little bow.

Literally, the heavy stack of paperwork had a blue satin ribbon wrapped around it, tied in a perfect bow. She knew. She knew she was going to die and wanted to make damn sure he was held responsible. Her loathsome feelings for him surpassed her death. It was almost too good to be true.

It was going to take weeks to go through all of it. To get it in order and build a case good enough to take to the judge for an indictment was going to be a daunting task. What they needed was the coroner's final report and for Heath to confess.

And yet, something still felt off.

***

Ben sat in a cold room on a round iron and concrete seat. It felt like he'd been waiting forever.

He leaned against the cement desk-like table that stretched from one end to the other, cutting the room in half; the other side was kept from view except what was directly in front of the visitor. At that moment it was a blank white wall.

He was the fourth one down in a row of ten with barely enough room to accommodate people. Once seated, he could have leaned back against the wall had he wanted to. There were partitions on either side of him and a few people who were already speaking to their incarcerated family members. He couldn't see them but heard their low voices as they tried to protect their privacy in a room specifically made to infringe on that particular right.

He looked down at the scratches in front of him. Names, a star, and random lines were all etched in layers of old paint that he could peel off, like others had done before him as they waited. Probably with nervous fingernails and nothing else to do. He drummed his fingers and chewed the skin around his thumb.

The black phone he was to use was on his right; wire ran through the thick window in front of him and crisscrossed, making a diamond pattern. He was distracted; it felt like a scene from a movie. It didn't feel real.

The sound of keys clanked, and then a heavy door slammed. And suddenly Heath was there, sitting across from him.

His father, the man who killed his mother and tried to kill him.

Ben wanted to run from the room but sat fused to his seat. He couldn't move.

Long after Heath had picked up the black phone with the silver coil wrapped around the cord, Ben couldn't move.

They stared at each other through the glass for an eternity before Ben put the receiver to his ear. No words passed between them for another few moments. No greeting, no speeches.

Ben broke the silence first.

"You know, I've been thinking about what I

would say to you for days, but now that I'm here, I've realized you aren't worth it. You do not deserve my time or attention, and I know anything that comes out of your mouth would be a lie. Dad, we know everything. Mom knew she was being followed; she knew you were going to have her killed. She spent months building a case against you and preserving each piece of evidence so there would never be a question of who did it."

Ben looked down at his shaking left hand and firmly flattened his palm across someone's curious artwork of a smiley face. Tears were already building up, and his throat was constricted. He looked at the man he had known all of his life in an oversized orange top, and he looked like a different human.

Heath's shoulders were slumped forward, his face unshaven, with dark sagging circles under his eyes. His hair looked greasy, and for the first time, as he put his head down, Ben saw that he was balding at the crown. He looked tired, old, and haggard. But mostly, he looked frightened and defeated. No arrogance; not solid, not confident, not drunk.

As Ben started listing the plethora of the evidence found, he could tell his father hadn't been told yet. He watched the once big, larger-than-life, obnoxious man shrink. The more Ben said, the smaller Heath seemed. Still holding the phone to his ear, Heath hung his head and started to sob.

Wilted; he looked *wilted.*

Ben wanted to ask why. *Why?* But for some reason he didn't.

There was no answer Heath could possibly give him that would make him understand or bring his mother back.

The pleasure Ben thought he'd feel seeing his father realize his mother had outsmarted him was nowhere to be found. There was no satisfaction in it; she was still gone, and he only felt anger, hate, and disgust.

Through it all, Heath never said a word. No remorse, no reaction except sadness with the realization that he was caught. The *only regret he had was getting caught.* His life was over.

Ben wiped his nose on the back of his shirt sleeve and hung up the receiver. Knowing his father could no longer hear him, he said,

"Goodbye, *Dad.*"

Ben left that day without an apology. He was positive that his father would try to make a deal and confess. He really didn't have a choice.

Allison had made sure of it. How proud he was of her.

As he made his way to his car, he realized losing his only living parent wasn't a loss at all. He was never there to begin with.

He thought of him as a smudge—a stain that tainted his whole life. Every memory that contained Heath was a bad one.

Heath was dead to him.

Twenty

Shultz entered a bar a few miles from the precinct.

It was dark and hazy, and it took a minute for his eyes to adjust. He scanned the room.

A few people were having a pitcher of beer and throwing darts. A woman sat at one of the digital poker machines; she looked way too invested. He noticed all bar stools were empty as he walked up.

"Hey Pete. I'll have a double Jack Daniels, neat."

He pulled bills from his pocket, put them on the bar, and waited for his bourbon.

The spot was a frequent hangout for cops, judges, lawyers, jailers, and people who were involved in the criminal justice system. It was a hole in the wall where they could go and "discuss' evidence, outcomes, and perps.

It was better than deciding someone's fate over a friendly golf game. Nine or nineteen holes; it didn't matter. It all still seemed shady to him. The unspoken predetermination of someone's future based on who knows who and how well their game was played.

Music was playing low on the jukebox...*go on, take the money and run*—how apropos.

He looked over his shoulder and saw Williams already seated in the only booth in the place. Shultz ordered him a Sam Adams draft before paying and joined him at the table. They were both early.

Shultz greeted his partner by his first name. Something that seemed to happen naturally when they were in a social setting.

"Garrett."

Williams answered,

"Dave."

He slid the pint towards his partner, and they sat and waited together for the coroner.

Williams was shelling boiled peanuts, eating each one individually before he grabbed another. Shells and skins were scattered around the space in front of the bowl.

They were lost in their own thoughts when the door opened. They both squinted against the intrusive sunlight, knowing immediately who it was that was walking in.

Craig Burns was an extremely large, overbearing man. He habitually ducked in doorways because of his height. His barrel chest and thick physique made him appear as wide as he was tall. He didn't walk; he shuffled.

Nice enough guy. He had been the county coroner for longer than Shultz had been on the force, and he wore the fatigue of the job like a badge of honor.

Inside the morgue, wearing a stained and wrinkled lab coat, he looked like a completely different person than he did in the real world.

Usually dress pants, button-down, tie, and fedora; old school. Still dressing the way his long-gone wife would have preferred. Or maybe that is just the way men in his generation felt appropriate. Their sense of style was stunted or lost when the career mattered more than fashion and they were no longer in love.

Two months were left before his dream of retiring to his boat and fishing all day—every day—for the rest of his life would become a reality. He really wasn't in a hurry to do anything anymore. Taking his time was part of his style. He walked slow, talked slow, ate slow, and even worked slow. That was never going to change.

All eyes were on him as he grabbed a beer and finally made his way to the table, choosing to pull a chair up instead of trying to size himself down to fit in the little booth.

The three men took turns shaking hands and greeting one another across the table and then fell silent.

They all knew why they were there, and as eager as the detectives were, they didn't rush him. They let him swig his beer and watch the television above the dartboards for a bit. Knowing from experience that he would speak when he was ready, they patiently waited.

He was unreadable.

Williams yelled to Pete, then pointed to their table, making a circular motion with his index finger, indicating they needed another round.

Craig took off his hat and placed it on the table, top side down. He was hunched over, rolling the label off of his beer bottle. Uncomfortable in his silence.

Shultz remembered a time when they would meet, and the conversation revolved around how their families were. They used to talk at length about wives, children, grandchildren, or recent vacations. Those days were long gone. Now they were three men with either death or at least one failed relationship. Work had become their lives, and it seemed there was a notable wedge or emptiness in their conversation; regret had taken the place of the younger, happier chitter-chatter. None of them knew what to say anymore if it didn't involve a case. Everything seemed to be a touchy subject.

After the round of drinks had been delivered, Craig stopped peeling the label long enough to speak, but he didn't look up.

"Fellas, this case..."

He cleared his throat, leaned back in his chair, and spoke to the air above him as he started again.

"This case—the outcome. It's the first one in a long time that had me stumped. I'm afraid my final decision is not going to be one you will be happy about."

Williams immediately sat up and began to speak; Shultz raised his hand to his partner.

"Let him finish."

And then Craig said the *one thing* they did *not* want to hear.

"Undetermined."

After the dreaded word "undetermined" was said out loud, they breathed out a sigh in unison. It was as though they had been holding their breath for weeks.

Williams interlaced his fingers and popped them; Shultz knew he was biting his tongue.

All of the evidence they had that supported Allison being murdered by her husband, and now the most important part, the professional they counted on to put on the stand to *make their case,* had decided to exclude himself from the team that needed him the most. The coroner was no longer their key witness.

Sure, they had enough to prove Heath's guilt in court for Allison's murder, Ben's attempted murder, and a laundry list of other grievances, but they *needed* him to agree the ashes in the trunk were hers. It really was next to impossible to get a conviction without a body or confession. They would have to go on what they had.

The circumstances of the case would leave a lot of loose ends, to include no one benefiting. Insurance doesn't pay out on "undetermined," and her son would have to wait years to touch one dime.

Craig spoke again.

"Listen; I don't like this any more than you do. I tried, but even with the bloody, half-burnt towel and the mound of melted gold and emeralds, there was not enough bone left to be sure. If it was her in that trunk, I have to have solid DNA results to prove it. I don't think either of you really needs my opinion on this. We are all familiar with this scenario; no teeth were found at the scene—this had to be a mob hit."

"I am sorry, fellas; this is as far as I go. My conscience won't allow me to feel sorry enough for her son to stick it to her asshole husband without concrete proof. No matter how much I'd like to. I'll leave that job for you two."

With that, Craig grabbed his hat, shook each of their hands, and walked out. The door slammed loudly behind him.

The slam felt like a punctuation mark, an exclamation point, or an insult. The end. No more waiting.

There was relief in that, even if it was the opposite of what they wanted to hear. They could and would build a solid case.

Shultz downed his drink and held it up high to let Pete know he needed another.

Williams held his glass with both hands and tapped his finger on the rim. After a few minutes of looking at Craig's empty chair and the full beer he'd left behind, the finality of the decision and what was ahead of them hit him.

He almost mumbled the words.

"Goddammit."

Shultz replied,

"We'd better get to the jail and interview Parker before the news makes headlines.

After Ben's visit, he should be beside himself right about now. Prime time for a confession."

Williams shrugged, looking a bit defeated or tired. His partner wasn't sure which.

They lingered a little longer, digesting the news and altering their mindset.

***

Before they could get to the county lock-up the next morning, it was too late.

Within hours of Ben's visit, Heath Parker had supposedly hung himself with his bedsheet.

A sniveling narcissistic greedy menace, who died exactly as a coward of his caliber would. He avoided any possibility of being held accountable... to include breathing.

***

Twenty-One

Ten days later, Leo returned from the city with the news of both the coroner's decision and Heath's suicide.

Allison stood in front of the kitchen window while Leo told her and waited for a reaction.

There really wasn't one.

She turned to him and asked,

"What does this mean? I mean, it's no surprise to me that Heath would kill himself rather than live with the consequences of getting caught, and honestly, the only thing I'm feeling is that the world just got a little bit better without him in it; but what about the coroner's statement? What does this mean for *us*? What do we do now?"

Leo stood, crossed one leg over the other, folded his arms, and rested against the counter. He was rubbing his beard with his fingers and thumb, like a wise old Chinese man would do. He stared at her curiously.

She guessed he was waiting for whatever response he had expected from her over the death of her husband, and the one she gave wasn't it.

Allison fidgeted a bit with the washcloth before folding it and laying it over the edge of the sink. Leo knew she was holding back. There was something she was keeping from him. He let it go, knowing if it was important enough, she would tell him.

He cleared his throat and answered her.

"They didn't get paid, Heath is dead, and they don't have a body to prove I held up my end of the bargain. The coroner's ruling will either appease them or it won't. They will accept that I did what I promised and chalk it up to bad luck, or it will make them suspicious, and they will come looking for me *and you*. I can't say. What I *can* say is that I am not going to stick around to see. If they figure out that you are alive, they will come after both of us—on principle alone."

He walked to his duffel bag on the table and started to remove items from his trip. The first thing out of the bag was bottles of vanilla linseed oil.

She watched him, thinking about what she had just been told. Both of her arms were bent behind her and propped up against the sink, one knee cocked up, her foot resting on the lower cabinets.

Leo listed each thing out loud as he removed it: two pairs of jeans, a coat, a few shirts, a sweater, panties, bras...

Even though he brought her *own* clothes from the house, and she should have been delighted to wear something other than his sweatpants or her workout gear, Allison was too lost in her thoughts to pay attention.

Until he pulled out a box of hair color.

She strolled over and picked the box up, turning it over to see the results of that color tinted on blond hair; she chuckled.

"You chose Auburn? *Auburn. Really, Leo?*"

He looked at her; she was amused. He didn't understand until she said,

"I have become the main character of every single bad "on the run" or "spy" movie I have ever seen! You must be kidding me. I'm a cliche."

He laughed with her for a minute before reminding her that, as far as the world was concerned, she was Bridgette Marie Robertson, and according to her passport, she indeed had brown hair. He just couldn't make himself buy a darker color.

She stopped laughing and asked,

"Shall I cut it?"

"That is entirely up to you. Unlike me, you do

have a choice."

"Oh no, Leo, don't cut your hair!"

He grinned and pushed a stray blond strand behind her ear.

"I am Edward Wayne Robertson, a property and real estate developer. I need to blend in. I'll do what I need to so I don't draw unnecessary attention to either of us."

He kissed her forehead and told her to get ready; they would have to leave by the end of the day.

"What about Lucky?" she asked.

Leo filled his cheeks with air and blew it out slowly before answering.

"I'm not sure yet; I was hoping you would have an idea. There is a family-owned farmhouse out on the main road. That seems like a good place to start."

Allison headed to the chair and picked up the sleeping pup. She put him in her lap and softly petted him. She cooed,

"It's going to be okay, little guy; I promise."

***

Sometime after noon, Allison emerged from the bathroom as a brunette. She hadn't left the color on as long as the instructions suggested and shampooed twice to tone it down. She wrapped it in a towel and went to check on Leo.

He was in the smaller bathroom attempting to cut his own hair in the reflection of an old hand-held mirror hung on the wall. She watched his frustration for a minute before covering her mouth to stifle a laugh.

"Here, let me help; I did raise a son."

She put her palm out, looked at the scissors in his hand, and nodded for him to have a seat in one of the kitchen chairs.

"How short?"

Leo shrugged. He had already cut uneven blocks out of it.

Allison detested having to trim even one curl on his head. She pulled it into a ponytail, inhaled deeply, exhaled loudly and said,

"Okay, here goes."

She held his severed mane in her hand for a minute, admiring it before setting it down on the table.

As Allison stood in front of him, snipping years of growth off of his head, she cried; she was cutting his hair through tears.

He grabbed her around the waist.

"It's just hair, sweet girl; it will grow back. Or am I ugly now?"

She slapped his shoulder for teasing her and laughed.

"No, never. But you are not allowed to cut it again after today. Ever!"

By the time Leo put his head down for her to clean up and shape his neck with the clippers, there was a mounded moat of black curls on the floor around him.

"There; done! Honestly, I didn't think you could get more handsome, but you look amazing!"

She grabbed the mirror off of the wall as he brushed hair off of his legs and shoulders.

When he looked at himself, he gasped. Short on the sides, back, and crown; a bit longer in the front. She combed his curls into waves that showed off his widow's peak.

There, in the mirror, staring back at him, was an almost exact replica of his brother. He looked just like him. It was astonishing. When he didn't immediately say anything, Allison said,

"You don't like it?"

"No, I do. Really."

He ran his fingers through the top, then down the side; the short stubble felt weird.

"I feel strangely naked." He said, smiling.

"Well, you look sexy."

"You think so, huh?"

Leo reached out and pulled her onto his lap. He released her hair from the towel, exposing her reddish-brown locks.

"*Wow*. You don't look so bad yourself. Beautiful. It suits you, really. You are stunning."

He had a piece of her hair in his hand, rubbing it between his fingers as he kissed her.

Leo swatted her on the behind, stood up, and set her firmly on her feet.

"We have a lot to do; let's get to it!"

She watched him running his hand across the back of his newly shaved neck as he headed down the hall toward the bedroom. Allison followed him, curious as to what he was going to do. She had already wiped every inch of the bathroom down with bleach.

Pausing just inside the doorway, she observed him beginning the task of removing all of the hardware from the footboard—the cuffs and chains that used to hold her hostage. She reached him before he could turn around and protest, encircled him from behind, and blindly slid her hands to the button of his jeans.

He grabbed Allison's hand, spun around, and pulled her onto the bed.

They shared a passionate kiss before quickly removing their clothes. A flurry of activity fueled by desire.

She stopped to gaze at him; he looked like a different person. He could have easily been an executive of a corporation or a trust fund baby.

Specks of freshly cut hair dotted his neck and earlobe. She kissed his clavicle and whispered to him,

"Tie me up."

"What?"

Eye contact made it twice as hot when she repeated it.

"I want you to put me back in shackles. Tie me to the bed again. I want you to."

And he did.

It was passionate, a little kinky, and very satisfying. Their attraction was beautiful—nothing held back.

Afterward, they laid together.

Nestled against his chest, sexual appetite satiated, she began to speak.

"Leo, I did it."

"You did what?"

She rolled over on her back and said,

"All of it."

"All of *what?* I don't understand."

Leo eased away from her so he could look at her as she unloaded all that she had kept from him for months. She revealed the truth in its entirety, and what she had to say was absolutely astounding.

Twenty-Two

(The year leading up to her abduction)

The idea didn't come all at once, but it did come.

It isn't as if one day Allison just woke up and decided she needed to cause chaos. It took time—years, in fact.

Abuse, neglect, cheating—one thing after another. There was never the proverbial "straw that broke the camel's back." It just evolved naturally over time. The important thing to remember here is that it wasn't premeditated. It just happened.

In the beginning, she hadn't intended it to go so far. She laid the groundwork, and Heath did it to himself.

It was like setting a mousetrap and presenting it to a starving rodent. He wanted the cheese; he convinced himself that he *deserved the cheese.* He wasn't exactly "Algernon." It took him a bit longer than she'd anticipated, but he did start nibbling.

Each step he took led him down the path of destruction. She didn't plot and plan; she was simply an innocent bystander.

Well—until she wasn't.

And even *that* turned out to be in her favor.

Allison had a degree in business finance. She always loved numbers, the stock market, and Wall Street, and she was a natural at investing. Her father taught her all the ins and outs, and she listened.

Just because she got married doesn't mean she stopped keeping up with it. She was keenly aware of what was happening in America, the world, and most importantly, her own household. Heath assumed she was stupid, and she let him believe it—no convincing necessary.

That's the thing with narcissists; they get so wrapped up in their own well-being and lies that they stop paying attention to anything or anyone that isn't useful or already trapped in their web. They are fueled by greed and lust.

They don't have real friends, wives, or children; they have *tax deductions* and *beneficiaries.*

And so, it happened.

It was really a day like any other, marked only by the fact it had been raining for four straight days, and she had nothing to do but zone in on Heath's business affairs and where he focused his true loyalty and attention.

She noticed he was going into her studio.

Early in the morning or late when he came in. He had no interest in her hobby; her files were in her studio.

She wrote things down on paper and intentionally left them lying around. Her bank statements, investments, dividends, and commissions earned were all scattered about. And let's not forget about the inheritance.

She knew he was going to use the information; she knew he was involved in criminal activity. It was as easy as the breadcrumbs in *Hansel and Gretel*. She threw them down, and he gobbled them up.

At first it was a test to see if he would take the bait, and eventually he did—several times.

After months and multiple good outcomes, she raised the stakes. Heath felt untouchable. The more he made, the more he spent. Gambling, drugs, and whatever else he could get involved in to hobnob with the big bosses. He was picking up bad habits from those he was defending in court, and he was way in over his head.

That was Heath, always trying to be more than what he was. And what he was, was a small man with self-esteem issues going through a midlife crisis, made worse by the fact he chose a career that kept him at everyone else's beck and call. People like her husband were never satisfied. There was no pride in honest work for him, and he hated being the low man on the totem pole. Allison knew that.

When he felt the most comfortable in her ignorance and his abilities, she pulled the rug out from under him. More than once.

No need to hire a private investigator either. One night she simply followed him from the office to see who he was so devoted to. Eventually the other woman would come in handy.

It was shortly after she learned about Monique that Allison realized she was being followed.

A twist, yes, but nothing she couldn't handle.

She figured a few more weeks of looking over her shoulder and the gangsters would go away on their own after they killed Heath. She'd left out the paperwork for her new will to make sure he knew he wouldn't benefit from her death; guess he didn't get the memo. He did get the Dalcon spreadsheets, though. He used them for insider trading, like she knew he would.

The only other person involved was a man at the gym. Allison paid him well, gave him a note and Monique's address, and instructed him to slip the note under her door if she ever went missing. Panic would surely make the other woman go to the police.

All evidence pointed to Heath. Allison made sure it did.

It's funny how people who easily betray tend to surround themselves with people who easily betray. Weakness is contagious.

It became quite comical for her to watch his undoing after months of his secret false "success." She'd be lying if she said she didn't relish every minute of it.

The only problem was that she hadn't counted on getting abducted. But as it turned out, she would still be headed to Sweden. To her homes, accounts, and fortune. Just a little later, and not alone.

She had outsmarted her husband and in return gotten everything Heath tried to steal. And somewhere in the midst of all of it, she fell in love. The kind of love her parents shared. And that was all she ever wanted.

Hidden inside the watch Leo retrieved from her son's safe was the chip she needed to access all Swedish accounts. She was an extremely rich woman.

Once they made it out of the USA—if they made it out of the USA—they would never have to worry about anything or anyone.

Ever again.

***

When she finished explaining all of the details, all of the little nuances, and things that had to fall into place for her plan to work... *wow*.

It was none other than genius.

Leo lay on his back with his forearm over his eyes. He'd had them closed while she spoke.

And after she told him everything, he told her the whole story of how he'd murdered a man to keep her son safe.

There were no secrets left.

The person she loved most in the world was alive because of Leo.

They embraced and stayed for a while, marveling at one another's strength. Loving each other even more.

Twenty-Three

Ben was an emotional man. Not excessively, but compared to others, absolutely.

He spent much of his life ignoring his gut and getting his feelings hurt or being surprised at the actions of others.

So, when Jake told him about the Linseed oil, he paid attention to his inner voice. The gnawing in his stomach wouldn't let him rest. He *knew* deep down to his core that his mother was alive. Or maybe it was hope?

He was convinced that he would *feel it* if she were dead.

He sat in front of the gallery in his car the day the order was supposed to be picked up. For ten hours, no one came. He waited for two more days in the parking lot. On the last day, as he almost dozed, it paid off.

Jake put the bottles into the stranger's hands himself and then called Ben with a description of the customer. A man such as Leo was easy to spot.

He saw him come outside. Watched him get

into a Jeep Renegade, adjust the rear-view mirror, and pull out.

Ben started his car and said, "here we go," as he followed him out and onto the main road.

***

Allison never told Leo she loved him, nor did he to her.

Saying the words somehow made them less important. From past experience, once those words were said, and each time they were heard, they lost importance. It cheapened them.

As they cleaned up around the house, the words played over and over in her mind. *I love you; I love you; I love you.* Except with Ben, it was not something she was comfortable saying.

She thought back over her marriage and couldn't remember one time telling Heath she loved him. She never liked to lie.

What if Leo didn't feel the same way?

Realizing it was pride and a past of nonreciprocal energy when it came to her and the most important people in her life, she decided she would tell him. She would tell him as soon as she was finished cleaning every crevice of the kitchen. No fingerprints, no personal items, not even a hair could be left behind.

Mulling over how she was going to say it and the many different responses he could possibly give, she was preoccupied. She paused in front of the kitchen window and realized it would be the last time she would enjoy that particular corner of the earth.

Snow still covered the ground in a thin blanket. Hazy Sun fought with huge billowing clouds for a place to shine. The trees were still bare, and half-brown limbs and trunks dotted the line of the forest. She'd painted it for its beauty, and she tried to imagine what it would look like when taken over by spring. When green would replace white.

Lost in thought, she almost didn't notice Lucky running across the big open space. Allison laughed as he suddenly dropped and rolled around on his back, feet in the air, kicking.

The dog lay still for a moment, staring at the sky. Maybe the quick, fluffy clouds had captured his attention. She leaned forward against the window and looked up to see what Lucky found so interesting. Then she looked to the right and saw Leo changing the plates on the Jeep. He was so clever.

When Leo was done, he came back in the house to get their bags.

The fireplace was blazing, and they had been throwing anything and everything into it all afternoon. If it wasn't going with them or it couldn't be washed to remove evidence, it got burned. To include her recently finished oil painting.

She absentmindedly removed her rubber gloves to throw into the fire when something—or rather, someone—caught her attention. She moved back to the window.

Maybe her eyes were playing tricks on her. It looked like a person coming toward the cabin. A man. Yes, she was sure of it.

She couldn't move; it was as if her blood had been replaced with cement. How firmly she was planted in the spot, unable to budge.

The gloves dropped to the floor and she screamed.

"LEO! *LEO!*"

On wobbly, fearful legs, Allison ran for the door.

***

Ben followed Leo all of the way to the main road. He passed him as he turned onto the nondescript lane as to not raise suspicion, then Ben circled back and parked. He walked for hours up the dirt road, and just after dawn, he spotted the Jeep and the cabin.

He watched the house from the forest edge until afternoon and then crept quietly around to the back. The window was high and covered in a blanket. There was a hole in one of the panes. The breeze blew it inward, creating a small sliver around the edge that he could see into if he stood on his tiptoes.

Then he saw him. The man from the gallery, and there was someone else in the room with him. Ben rolled a small log close enough to stand on and got a better look.

A woman—there was a woman. He held his breath and waited for the breeze to blow the window cover in again.

The woman had her arms above her head, but he couldn't make out details. He heard clanking; the sound was rhythmic. *Clank, clank, clank.* And then quicker.

The next breeze blew long enough to see that the woman had brown hair. The sound came from handcuffs against a wrought iron headboard. She was not there willingly.

Ben stepped down from the log and started to retreat back into the woods.

Until he heard her say,

"Please."

Despite hearing only one word, Ben recognized his mother's voice even through the glass window. He stopped dead in his tracks, turned back around, and climbed up again.

The next breeze—just a flicker of her face beyond the man's ribcage—left no doubt.

It *was* his mother.

Tears stung his eyes. He all but fell down from the stump and darted to the forest.

"Think, Ben; think."

His cellphone had no service; there was no way to call for help.

His mother was still alive, still being held captive, and she was being raped, begging for her release. The realization was too much. How many times? What had she endured?

Ben walked and then ran until he couldn't hold it in anymore. He vomited. The heat from his bile melting away the snow enough to see foliage underneath. He stood with his hands on his bent knees, focused on the newly uncovered leaves and dirt, until the nausea passed.

Again, he tried his phone; still no service.

He slid down the rough edge of a cedar and sat on the cold ground. Tears streamed down his face. He shook his head in disbelief. The gun rested across his knees; he ran his fingers across the barrel, then hugged it against his chest. He had to do something, and he had to do it alone.

He was sleep deprived, thirsty, and in total turmoil. He wasn't the strong one, and he deeply regretted not allowing Jake to come with him. That was a mistake.

Ben sat for a while under the safety of cover while he tried to decide what to do. Just before dusk, he heard conversation and activity.

Timidly, he worked his way through thick brush until he had a view of the front yard. The man was going in and out of the house carrying suitcases to the open waiting doors of the Jeep.

Ben didn't see his mother. He wasn't sure if she was about to be moved or killed. So he stayed crouched down and watched.

A dog was following the man, playfully nipping at his pant leg. The subject of his attention (Leo) never made a noise and seemed preoccupied and in a hurry. If Ben was going to act, he needed to do it quickly.

Just as he had settled his nerves enough to confront the abductor, someone seemed to beat him to it.

An intruder came from woods closer to the road. He was wearing light camouflage, his gun already drawn, and he seemed to be looking straight at Ben. Was he part of the kidnapper's crew? Had he seen him?

Panic set in, but only for a moment as Ben realized he wasn't looking at *him* at all.

The man curved around the vehicle until the large man holding a suitcase was in full view. He spoke angrily and vengefully. Russian?

It was a split-second choice.

Ben jumped from his spot and started shooting at the camouflaged man. One step, pull the trigger; two steps, pull the trigger. Ben walked and fired without thinking—three shots, four shots, five shots. The camouflaged man was on the ground, bleeding. Ben got closer, firing two more.

Immediately he turned from camouflage man to his mother's rapist and fired several shots in succession. He squeezed the trigger again and again, but after the first loud bang, there were only clicks. *Click. Click. Click. Click.*

The gun was empty. His ears were ringing.

Leo slid down the Jeep and held his side, blood oozing through his fingers. He looked up at Ben, who was pointing an empty weapon at him, his hand shaking wildly.

Allison was screaming.

"No! Oh my God, *no! Oh God,* Benjamin, stop! *Please stop!*"

Ben's hand dropped to his side; he released his grip, and the weapon fell to the ground with a thud.

Allison ran to Leo and held him. In between sobs, she repeated,

"No, *no, no.* You can't die. Leo, *Leo, I love you, please—you can't die!*"

Leo smiled weakly, coughed, winced in pain, and then answered,

"I love you too. Hello, Ben; a pleasure to finally meet you."

Ben looked at Leo. He repeated his name a few times out loud. A foggy memory crept in. The picture was vague and hazy, like a dream, but definitely familiar. He recalled the night that someone shot a man in his living room. A wave of regret washed over him.

Allison gave a quick pleading glance at her son before trying to help Leo. With his arm over her shoulder, they managed to get back into the house.

After one last look at the dead man bleeding out in the snow, Ben followed them in with Lucky close behind. Though completely confused and astounded, he followed them anyway. He was exhausted.

Twenty-Four

Ben drove toward Washington in the middle of the night down winding roads. His shoulders and arms ached. His mind raced. He'd shot two men; one was dead and he had no idea if the other would survive. The events weighed heavily on him, but he left Leo in Allison's capable hands and hoped for the best.

Adrenaline still coursing, he was wide awake and a bit discombobulated.

He and his mother spent eight precious hours together; he wanted to focus on that.

"It was Leo all of this time, protecting me. Protecting my mother—*I shot him.*"

He kept repeating it, in disbelief. But it was true; all of it had *really* happened.

They buried the hitman in a shallow grave deep in the woods. Should he ever be recovered, his body would bear Leo's identification. The bullets that killed him came from a gun registered to Jake. However, it was unlikely that anyone would ever find him, and they would all be long gone by then.

For decades at a time, those forests remained untouched.

Leaning back in the driver's seat, Ben thought of all the things his mother told him. He laughed out loud and, like he'd done on hundreds of *ordinary* days past, absentmindedly turned on the radio.

Brilliant; his mom was brilliant.

He grinned with the new awareness that everything he needed was contained in the watch he'd worn for almost a year.

His mother and he decided on the perfect rendezvous spot to meet in six months' time for a fresh start, and he was giddy.

Lucky, who'd been asleep in the passenger seat, woke, stretched, and yawned. He reached over and patted the little guy's head. The feel of the pup's soft fur was soothing.

His mom was alive; he was a very rich man, and he was going home.

He sang along to Steve Miller Band's *Take the money and run*, with the last two "*whoo, whoos*" being obnoxiously loud.

Ben pumped his fist in the air with excitement and screamed, "*YEEESSS!*" He pounded a few times on the steering wheel and then sped up. He couldn't wait to get home and tell Jake.

For once, Heath Parker got beaten at his own sick game. The happiness that came with that knowledge was enough to last the rest of Ben's life.

***

Monique was drawn to Heath's funeral by a force she could not understand and obviously couldn't ignore. Something inside of her had to attend; she needed the finality of it.

As she stood and observed from a distance, her heels kept sinking into the soft ground. She awkwardly held her free hand against a tree for balance, waiting—for what felt like an eternity—hoping that the service would be over soon and she would be able to move closer to the casket.

There were no last words to say, or anyone to *say them to*, for that matter. She had no intention of dramatically throwing a flower onto the coffin as it was lowered down to the dirt, like so many cliché American movies she'd seen—and besides, she hadn't even brought flowers.

Monique really had no idea what she'd been thinking when deciding to go and hadn't considered anything past the point of being present. There were only about ten people gathered, none of whom she had ever met.

Lighting a cigarette, she leaned against the trunk and checked the time. The taxi had the meter running. Highly aware of cost, she prematurely snubbed out her smoke with the toe of her shoe, pulled her coat around her shoulders, and gave up entirely on the thought of getting any kind of closure.

As she got into the cab, no one seemed to notice. For the first time in her life, she felt invisible. Not sure if it was her new invisibility or the very real feeling of loss over the only man she'd ever loved, but an unexpected tear trickled down her cheek—and Heath didn't even deserve that one.

She wiped it away with the back of her gloved hand, sniffled, and cleared her throat. Avoiding the gaze of the driver in the rearview mirror, she numbly stared out the window.

The trip from the cemetery was short, and she arrived at her small, elegant flat just past noon. She made a mental note to *thank God* for small favors.

The gas had already been cut and it was freezing inside. Another mental note was made to *curse God* for her situation.

First kicking off her pumps, then delicately removing her black velvet funeral hat, she swapped them out for a warm toboggan and fuzzy house shoes. Her coat stayed on as she headed to the kitchen island, uncorked a bottle of red and poured herself a glass. It was only then that she noticed.

She slid the wine glass across the counter as she took a seat on a barstool. For a moment, all she could do was stare at a rather large manila envelope that had somehow made its way into her home during the short period of time she'd been gone.

Monique's eyes cautiously swept around her kitchen and then all spaces within view.

Nothing—no sound, not a thing out of place; nowhere for someone to hide. Convinced she was alone, but more than a little spooked, she reached for the package. No label, no postage.

Taking a deep swig of liquid courage, she struggled to break the seal, sustaining a paper cut in the process. "*Ouch!*"

Sucking the droplet of blood from the top of her cold thumb, she used her other hand and dumped the contents onto the bar.

Stunned, Monique emptied her glass in one long gulp. Eyes wide, she stood and surveyed the apartment a second time. And again, *she saw no one.* Just her and the wild heartbeat pounding in her ears. She nervously wiped both of her hands down her coat; her palms were suddenly sweating. She approached the contents again and took into account all that was lying there.

Two large banded stacks of cash, one in Euros, the other in USD. One loose gold women's watch, and lastly, a folded piece of yellow legal paper simply marked, **READ.** Her hand trembled as she reached out to touch the money.

Climbing back up onto the barstool, she poured herself another drink as she took a closer look at the watch: expensive, gold, classy—Cartier.

Puzzled, she unfolded the note.

Miss Laurant,

Enclosed you will find everything you need, or shall I say, all that is due to you. He made more than one person's life agony. It's okay to feel hurt and scared, just don't get stuck in it; you have a life to live.

When you reach France, do take this watch to a jeweler in Paris. The small shop next to the hotel you and Heath enjoyed last year, remember? Ask for Jaque; he will be waiting for you.

All that you need for the life you've always dreamed of is inside this envelope.

Take care of yourself. Enjoy; you deserve it.

Sincerely

— Anonymous B.

She read the words several times before lighting a cigarette. She picked up the letter, set the corner on fire, and watched as the flame enveloped the whole sheet. She dropped it into the ashtray, mesmerized by its complete ruin into ashes. Another mental note: *thank God for Anonymous B.*

She took out her large suitcase and frantically began to pack, but somewhere in the midst of the flurry she stopped and became still and *calm*.

She looked around at the pictures, the furnishings, and her wardrobe full of clothes, jewelry, and personal items.

Standing in the middle of the room, her hands resting at her sides, she spun, slower than molasses in January, a full three hundred and sixty degrees, zeroing in on several unique objects. None of which meant anything to her, not even trinkets of love gifted to her by *him*.

A choice was made.

She was ready to go a short time later, wearing Jeans, a sweater, a coat, and loafers, and not one ounce of hesitation.

Monique didn't give it a second thought or glance back as she rolled her small carry-on across the threshold to leave. Hell, she didn't even lock the door.

She opened her handbag for a quick last-minute inventory: passport, money, wallet... *check!*

She observed the time on her new watch, pausing longer than necessary; it still intrigued her. "*Right, I must hurry!*" She said the words aloud and immediately snapped back into the present. So excited at the thought of going home, *where* the money came from didn't matter.

She couldn't get out of the building quickly enough.

She had a plane to catch.

The End

JUST A FEW IMPORTANT THANK YOUS!

ACKNOWLEDGEMENTS:

I wouldn't have been happy with this book as it was. Listening to my readers has helped me immensely and given me cause to not just keep writing but *to do better*. A few of those special people are as follows: My mother, of course, but also a group of women who came together to support my work. Alicia Faught, Kenya Martin, Nina Vallee, Robin Martin, Jessica Lineberry, Alyssa Heuerman, Jessica palacio, and my cousins, Denise, Katy, Shannon, Misty, and Cindy. And finally, a huge appreciation for my editor/format expert and friend, Riyaz. I am overwhelmed with gratitude for each of you.

Please enjoy this sample of
BLOOMING AFTER THE BLAZE:
Three Years on the Run

Based on a true story...

CHAPTER 19
Tethered

Periodically, I go to the pyramids. There is a hostel there that has a perfect view of them. I go to the rooftop and meditate, enjoy the scenery, or just absorb the vibe.

"Vibe" is not a word I would have used two years ago, but I find in Egypt, I use it a lot. The energy here is indescribable. Even for someone who didn't used to believe in the everyday ebb and flow of it, it's impossible to ignore.

There's something about this place and those pyramids that will set a person's mind at ease while simultaneously questioning all. I believe it would make anyone give serious thought to the *why* in every single thing. From birth to purpose and everything in between.

So many of my years have been spent in the work, eat, and entertainment mentality of living here on Earth. I never really felt the need to consider anything else. Maybe because I could never slow down enough to catch my breath or ever had a chance to give into second guessing.

I look back and feel now that although I made all of the life-directing decisions concerning myself, each one was made as a result of another. I just adapted along the way, even at times when I shouldn't have.

In retrospect, I have been like a leaf in a river. Just floating downstream and having no real control or anything to hold onto. I might have gotten hung up on a rock or limb along the way, giving me a view of the stream and which direction would have been the most beneficial, but was never in that position long enough to see a clear picture or form a plan. The next current or wind would pick me up and carry me forward too soon, and I would just adapt and go with the flow. It was like,

"Oh, this is what we are doing now? Okay."

Then I would set about making the best of it.

However obvious it is to me now that I should have taken control to shift my mind and produce a more favorable outcome, I didn't have that knowledge then. I am pretty certain that even if I had, I would have lacked the courage.

When I came to Egypt, I was so wrapped up in seeing all of the tourist attractions. Taking pictures, and as most travelers do, running from one amazing historical site to another. All so that I could say, show, and commit to memory that I had been there. Which is comical to me now—the thought that I would ever forget *any* of this. I am not sure when it started to change, but it certainly did.

While I do still consider what I would like to see next, it's more about the experience of feeling and enjoying the rich and solid vibe. The vibration of this country is real. It is real and at times difficult to comprehend.

If you choose to make this country a must-see for yourself, you need to realize a few things first.

One of the most important things on that list is that if you come here with any silver dental work in your mouth, expect it to hurt. It will. As a matter of fact, I have had every single filling in my mouth either fall out or cause so much discomfort that I have had to have them all replaced.

Since my own experience, I've heard countless stories from other travelers along the same lines. There is no explanation, except that the vibration of this place is on a whole different level. Your body will actually start to reject anything that is unnatural or harmful.

Maybe I sound a bit crazy, and a few months ago, I would have felt anyone telling me this was a bit "touched." But it is a very real phenomenon.

I even saw a dentist before I came here and had a routine check-up and maintenance done to make sure I wouldn't have any issues. Still, not enough preparation and foresight.

When I walk through Giza or get close to the pyramids, there is an overwhelming power in the air. The hair on my arms and head stands up. As if it were statically charged. That isn't where it stops. The energy seems to rise up from my core, much like an excitement or adrenaline rush. It cannot be subdued. At first, I wasn't sure what was going on. It felt as if I was being overstimulated. I perceived it as nerves.

Lucid dreams of all aspects of my life were every-night occurrences, not just the one awful incident. I am not sure if anyone has ever written about this being part of the Egyptian experience, but I feel it is very important to relay.

I had to relocate and give myself more distance from that area until I could learn to grip that energy in a more effective and less mind-scrambling way.

The ground here is a Tesla ball, and all of us are walking on it, absorbing its life. When a person is new to it and not aware, it will feel disconcerting and nauseating.

Even if you do not consider yourself religious, Egypt is a spiritual place.

Again, I am not sure when it happened that I changed. At some point, instead of feeling like an individual or lone soul walking these deserts and streets, I started to feel connected. A connection to everyone and everything. Although I've never been here before, it all feels familiar. I do not feel alone, but instead feel that wherever I go and whatever I do, I do it with a crowd. Hypothetically, of course.

For the first time in my life, I don't feel disconnected or singular. It is as if everyone here has a cord connected to one another.

A better analogy would be a lightning bolt. A surge of electricity with all of its little tentacles of power, but instead of power connecting that energy, here—it's people.

It goes much deeper than that.

Not only are we all part of the same bolt, but somehow, we are all part of the source of the outburst of power. The part we cannot see—way up in the universe. I am tethered to something unseen, only felt. Even though I can walk away from a group and find myself alone, I never really am. I don't feel as if I am on a short leash, but one made with infinite expansion material. I can go as far as I want. It is my soul, heart, or energy that will always find its way back to others and the main source.

This feeling has a glorious side effect: safety. I feel safe.

These people have something inside of them different than any other humans I've lived around. They have a want and need to be a part of everyone and everything around them. With sincere effort on their part to connect as much as possible. They have grace and gratitude.

When I'd only been here a few months, my dentist asked me where I lived. I told him I lived in Indonesia. His reply surprised me.

He said that he had been there once and that he was not fond of it because the people were cold. He said he felt no real human connection. I didn't understand him having that opinion. I thought about that for days.

Mainly because I love that country, and compared to Americans, there is no lack of feeling their love. Now I realize that he was comparing it to here. If that is the case, I'm not so sure that every country wouldn't be a bit unfeeling and cold when put next to Egypt—perspective.

Even though most people here do not speak English, choosing instead to be fluent in French or even Russian, they *try* to communicate. They *want* to talk to me. These people *need* to feel human connection.

In the beginning, I didn't understand. I almost felt aggravated or put out when I realized Arabic is mostly all they speak. In my mind, this is a very touristy country. I didn't see selfishness in my expectation that they should all know English as a second language.

What I have come to realize is that the little bit of Arabic that I have learned to speak has built a bridge between me and them. A smile and a few words and we interact perfectly. Understanding each other goes beyond a fluent language. They focus on our commonality.

I feel it when they touch my arm as they slow down their speech trying to teach me. While I teach them the English version. They yank the smiles, love, and laughter straight out of my soul. It doesn't matter how busy they are; there is never an occasion that they do not make time for a smile, a wave, or a moment of showing their pleasure in my presence. It touches a place in my heart that I cannot completely understand myself.

It's an everyday, open exchange of our inner power and source. A dance of sorts between each and every living being in this country. I didn't have to decide to participate; the universe decided for me. It is truly the most eye-opening and marvelous thing I have ever experienced.

I had forgotten how to cry until I came here. Which I thought was strength, but I'd also forgotten how to feel true joy for life. The two go hand-in-hand. Pain and joy. You cannot truly experience one without the other. You learn depth of feeling when you learn to give into both. You must give each its turn, or you will never experience life the way it's intended.

I believe as humans we do ourselves such a huge injustice considering the way we view happiness. I myself have my own view, as I am sure everyone does.

When my son Fin was in high school and about to graduate, the senior class was interviewed and asked individual questions.

The question presented to him was something to the effect of who his hero was. Who motivated him the most? His answer was published in the newspaper the next day. I was unaware of its existence until a friend called me and told me to go grab a local paper.

So, I did.

I sat in my car scanning the pages for a clue as to why she would tell me to go out and buy one, and then I saw it.

In the middle section were pictures of some of the graduating students. When I spotted my son, under his picture, I read.

His answer to who his hero was? His mom. It was me.

He went on to say that I was strong and determined, and for that he looked up to me. This was—and remains to be—my definition of happiness. It is all the validation I should ever want or need. Through all that was going on in my life, no matter my struggles or failures, one of the main purposes in my life that kept me marching forward was watching. He saw me.

Not only did he see me, but he appreciated and valued me to such an amazing extent that he didn't care how lame it might have appeared to other young adults his age by making it known. Simply put, he loved me back.

I was so touched that I sat in my car and cried.

As wonderful as that feeling was and is, I will compare every other feeling of happiness I ever have to the minute I read that newspaper. I will, without intention, overlook happiness that doesn't measure up to that moment in time. The feeling of being loved by one that I love is what life is about. It doesn't mean I shouldn't truly appreciate all other forms of joy.

We must stop assigning different degrees to happiness. Any happiness is to be cherished and appreciated. There truly is always going to be another great heartfelt pleasure in our lives.

None greater than the next unless we deem it so in our own minds.

We limit ourselves. The love that brings joy and vice versa should be limitless. Each and every single second is a gift. Emotions those moments bring are to be included, not rated.

I walk around in the midst of these people as if I am wearing a space suit that is equipped with happiness, gratitude, and love pouring in and around me through a lifesaving tube. I simply cannot feel any other way.

I feel my soul in Egypt. I have found myself here.

*****

BE SURE TO CHECK OUT THESE OTHER TITLES

In this fiercely personal memoir, Jamie Lee Carrie invites you into a world marked by beauty and brutality, laughter and loss, silence and survival. From the suburbs of Texas to the rooftops of Egypt, she

weaves a story not just of pain—but of persistence. Not just of what was taken—but what still bloomed. Told with unflinching honesty and flashes of unexpected grace, *Blooming After the Blaze* is the true account of a woman who refused to stay broken. It's not a story about running from the past—it's about what you find when you finally stop and face it. It's faith, hard work, and resilience in real time, and it might just make you believe in yourself.

Some seeds only bloom after fire.

Where the Water Glows is an intriguing novel about the mysterious forces that bind us, the life-altering things we inherit without warning, and what love demands when the stakes are highest. Rich with atmosphere, it invites readers into a haunting and hopeful journey—one where miracles don't come with fanfare, and healing asks more of us than expected. With unforgettable characters and a setting that hums with quiet magic, this is a story that lingers long after the final page.

For decades, the *urban legend* made its way through Egypt, surrounding countries, and beyond. It had even captured the attention of the Nazi regime in the 1930s, and they tirelessly searched.

It was the tale of a young Egyptian prince born in the 1700's named Alaa. An arranged marriage, an eventual love that was all consuming—of a difficult pregnancy, an impossible birth, and the loss of both mother and child. Unimaginable pain and grief, and an elaborate tomb built into the side of a cliff in an undisclosed location in Cairo. The death of a king and an inheritance of **5 stones** that would allow five possibilities for redemption.

****

SOULMATES, REINCARNATION, FRIENDS TO LOVERS AND TIME TRAVEL. SET IN LONDON, SCOTLAND, AND EGYPT In 2019

NEW RELEASE
COMING SOON!

December 2025

© © *OLIVE'S ONUS*

Book design © Jamie Lee Carrie

ALL BOOKS AVAILABLE NOW
AT YOUR FAVORITE RETAILER
Also on B&N, Kindle, Apple read etc.

QR Code for Author
JAMIE LEE CARRIE

www.ingramcontent.com/pod-product-compliance
Lightning Source LLC
Chambersburg PA
CBHW010514100726

47903CB00009B/2743